SAINT JEAN sur ME

THE CHRONICLES OF A
FRENCH NARROW GAUGE RAILWAY

PETER SMITH

ISBN-13: 978-1533553959

ISBN-10: 1533553955

COPYRIGHT PETER SMITH 2016

CONTENTS.

INTRODUCTION

CHAPTER 1 THE ENGINE SHED

CHAPTER 2 THE CRANE

CHAPTER 3 SOMETHING IN THE MUD

CHAPTER 4 THE AUTORAIL

CHAPTER 5 DERAILMENT

CHAPTER 6 ROAST DUCK

CHAPTER 7 MADAME PINOT

CHAPTER 8 THE FILM

CHAPTER 9 CHICKENS

CHAPTER 1O A VISIT FROM 'LES ANGLAIS'

CHAPTER 11 FIRE & WATER

CHAPTER 12 THE HARBOUR MASTER MISSES LUNCH

CHAPTER 13 THE BULL

CHAPTER 14 THE AUTORAIL EXPIRES

CHAPTER 15 BASTILLE DAY

CHAPTER 16 THE AUTHIE RESTORED.

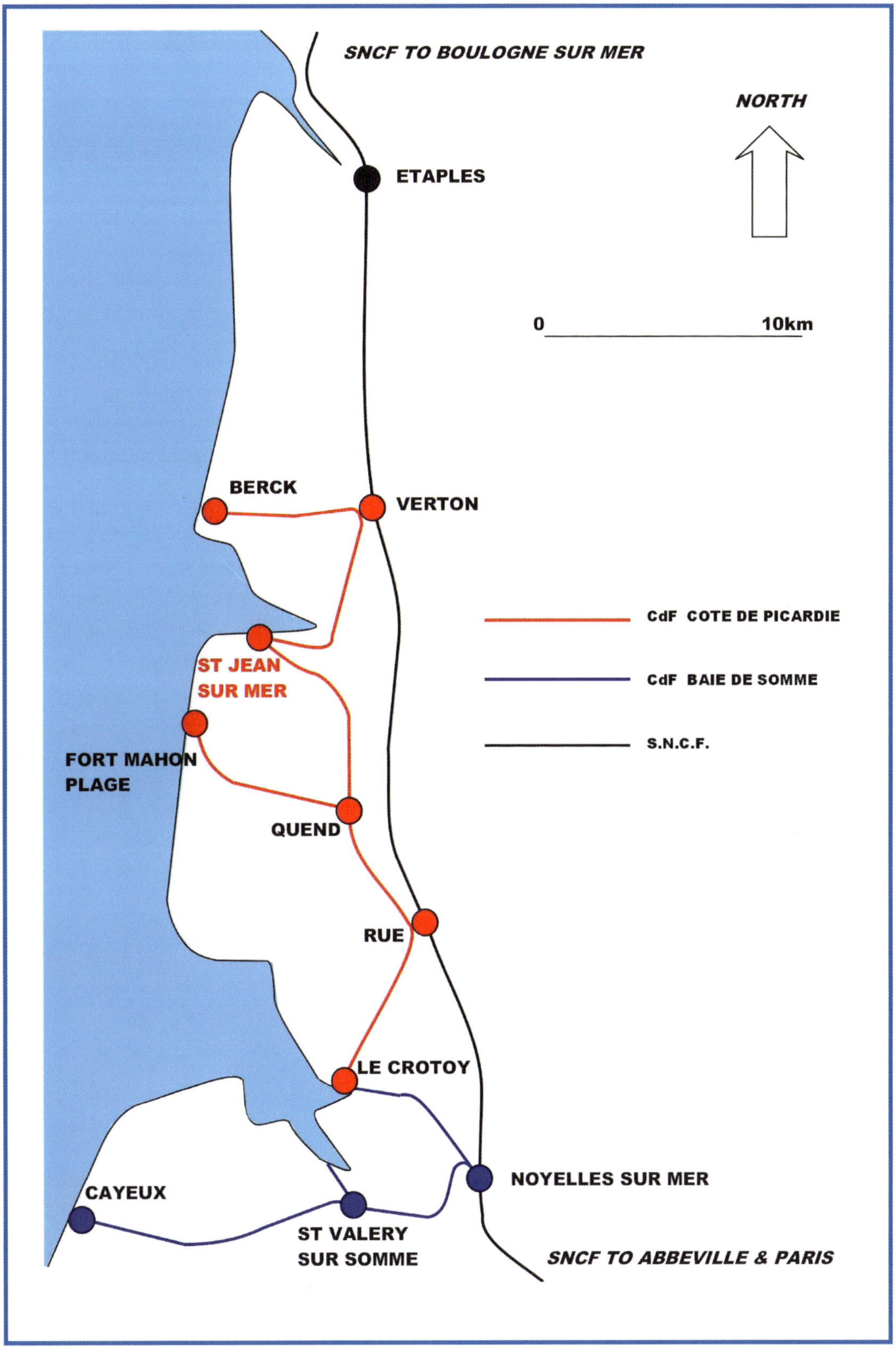
SNCF TO BOULOGNE SUR MER
NORTH
ETAPLES
0
10km
BERCK
VERTON
CdF COTE DE PICARDIE
CdF BAIE DE SOMME
S.N.C.F.
ST JEAN
SUR MER
FORT MAHON
PLAGE
QUEND
RUE
LE CROTOY
NOYELLES SUR MER
CAYEUX
ST VALERY
SUR SOMME
SNCF TO ABBEVILLE & PARIS

INTRODUCTION

If you follow the coast of France south from Boulogne sur Mer you will come to a wide estuary where the River Authie meets the sea, but try as you might you will not find a town called St Jean sur Mer on the south bank. The estuary of the Authie is a wild place, all mudbanks, reeds and wildfowl undisturbed by people other than the occasional hunter. The coast is developed to the north and to the south where there are wide sandy beaches but the Authie seems to be part of a forgotten world, bypassed by the modern age.

That is what you will find if you visit the area but this book creates an alternative reality in which the riverside was developed into a port and a town called St Jean sur Mer grew up on the south bank as early as the Roman period and continued to grow in medieval times into a prosperous harbour with a fishing fleet and as a stopping place for coastal trading vessels.

In due course, as was the case throughout France, the town felt the need to be connected to the rail network and as the main line of the Nord railway passed a few kilometres to the east a narrow gauge system was promoted by local people to serve the area, the Chemins de Fer de la Cote de Picardy. The railway had it's headquarters at Verton, where the Nord station was, but it served St Jean sur Mer where a little station was built in 1898 alongside the harbour wall. Trains reversed here before continuing their journey south to Le Crotoy and the connection with the Baie de Somme system, so St Jean was quite a busy place in a relaxed French narrow gauge sort of way.

This book is set in and around the station in the Summer of 1958, by which time only tourist traffic was keeping the company afloat and money was in short supply. The CdF Cote de Picardy kept going though, against all the odds….sometimes it even made a small profit.

I have taken terrible liberties with the railway geography of the Picardie coast area, but this is a work of fiction so reality needs to be disregarded for a while. Although the Baie de Somme railway was the inspiration for the book and all the places mentioned other than St Jean are real, none of the events described actually happened and all the characters are the product of my imagination.

THE HARBOUR

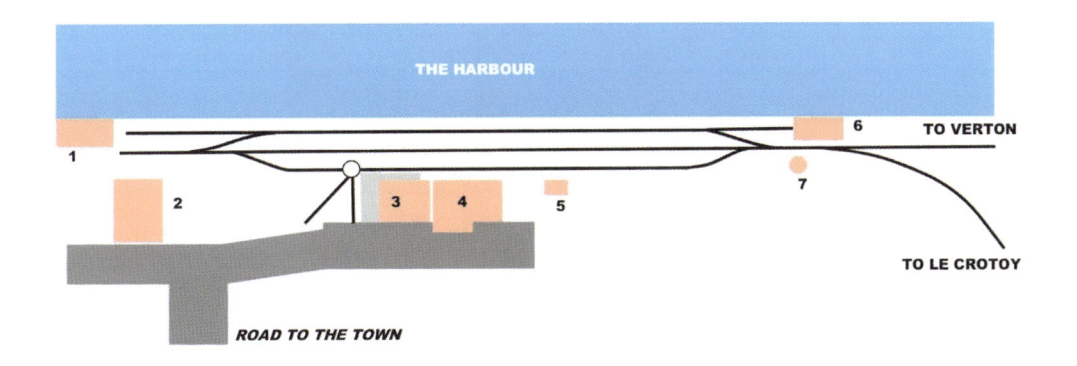

1. THE HARBOUR MASTER'S OFFICE
2. THE STATION CAFE
3. GOODS SHED
4. STATION BUILDING
5. TOILETS
6. ENGINE SHED
7. WATER TOWER

TO VERTON

TO LE CROTOY

ROAD TO THE TOWN

St Jean sur Mer station, with the Chef's office from which Jacques could see all the comings and goings on his station and in which he could hide when necessary!

The early years on the CdP. The line was opened with a fleet of Corpet Louvet 0-6-0 tank engines. The number 1, seen in the bottom picture, is the loco that would be preserved.

CHARACTERS:

JACQUES RODIN CHEF DE GARE St JEAN sur MER.

MARC ARTOIS SUPERINTENDANT, RESEAU DE COTE DE PICARDIE.

LOUIS THE LOCO DRIVER BASED AT ST JEAN SHED.

MAURICE HIS FIREMAN.

MADAME PINOT THECOMPANY BOOK KEEPER, AN ALARMINLGY EFFICIENT WIDOW.

MADAME JULES WORKS AT St JEAN STATION IN AFTERNOONS IN BOOKING OFFICE.

MADAME ARTUR. AS ABOVE, IN THE MORNINGS.

MARIE WORKS AT THE NURSERY, THE DAUGHTER OF MADAME ARTUR.

MARIANNE A SIXTEEN YEAR OLD GIRL WHO LIVES AT CAFE PICARDIE.

OLD CHARLES THE OLDEST FISHERMAN.

HENRI GOODS POSTER.

MICHEL GOODS PORTER.

A CRANE DRIVER

THE MAYOR OF St JEAN sur MER.

TIMETABLE OF St JEAN STATION.

08.30   DEPARTURE TO VERTON.

09.30 ARRIVAL FROM VERTON - DEPARTS FOR LE CROTOY AT 09.45.

10.00 ARRIVAL FROM LE CROTOY - DEPARTS FOR VERTON AT 10.30.

11.00 ARRIVAL FROM VERTON - DEPARTS FOR LE CROTOY AT 11.30.

11.30 ARRIVAL FROM LE CROTOY. - DEPARTS FOR VERTON AT 11.45.

11.55 ARRIVAL FROM VERTON - DEPARTS FOR LE CROTOY AT 12.10.

14.00 ARRIVAL FROM VERTON. - DEPARTS FOR LE CROTOY AT 14.15

14.45 ARRIVAL FROM LE CROTOY - DEPARTS FOR VERTON AT 15.00

16.00 ARRIVAL FROM VERTON - DEPARTS FOR LE CROTOY AT 16.15

16.30 ARRIVAL FROM LE CROTOY - DEPARTS FOR VERTON AT 17.00.

17.30. DEPARTURE FOR LE CROTOY; FORMS FIRST LE CROTOY DEPARTURE THE FOLLOWING DAY.

18.00 ARRIVAL FROM VERTON - LOCO PUT IN SHED, FORMS 08.30 DEPARTUERE THE FOLLOWING DAY.

JUNE, JULY & AUGUST ONLY;

19.00 ARRIVAL FROM VERTON, DEPARTS FOR LE CROTOY AT 19.15.

Chapter 1

THE ENGINE SHED

Nobody heard the engine shed fall into the harbour; at three o'clock in the morning St Jean sur Mer was fast asleep.

The following morning, though, that was a different matter - there was uproar! The storm that had been raging all night had begun to die down, and as the first fishermen ventured down to the quayside they soon realised that the dilapidated wooden shed that had been keeping the weather off the locomotives of the Reseau de Cote de Picardie was no longer there - just the concrete foundations and some splintered planks. The fisherman ran into the town to tell their families, they quickly threw on some clothes and rushed to tell their friends....... eventually some one even thought to pass on the amazing news to the 'Chef de Gare' himself.

The engine itself was still standing there, to be sure, standing where it always stood, but looking rather self conscious now as though it had been caught in the act of getting dressed for the morning and wasn't at all sure why all these people were staring at it. Open to the elements, it looked cleaner than it had looked for years with the rain gleaming on its paintwork. It seemed to have escaped pretty well unscathed, what's more, but the shed that last night had been sheltering it from the storm - well, the shed was gone, there was no doubt about it.

Jacques Rodin, Chef de Gare at St Jean sur Mer, stood on the harbour wall looking miserably into the still angry waves of the harbour as if somehow he could encourage the shed to jump back out of the water and onto its foundations. Stare as he might, though, nothing happened, and other than a few pieces of wood floating in the grey water nothing could be seen either. Jacques was an important man in St Jean; it was his misfortune that he didn't look important. He was shortish, stoutish, not a man you would notice if you passed him in the street. He liked the quiet life, the ordered life with no unpleasant surprises. Nothing like today, in fact.

Jaques spat into the waves, shrugged his shoulders, and began to walk back towards his office in the station from where he would have to telephone his boss at Verton, the junction with the SNCF and the outside world. He didn't know what he was going to say; if all else failed, he might have to tell the truth, and who on earth was going to believe that? Even the damn seagulls seemed to be laughing at him.

"Hey, Jacques, wait a minute will you........someone told me.............".

The voice tailed off as the early shift engine driver came round the corner of the station and looked to where his shed should have been. "Merde! What's happened to it?" cried Louis......"Where's my bloody shed gone?".

That was the question everyone was asking; by half past six the rain had stopped and most of the town seemed to be gathered on the quayside, but no one could add anything to what they already knew.......last night they'd had an engine shed, and this morning it was gone! Everyone had a theory, of course, everyone always does, but the fact was that the old engine shed had simply given up the ghost and blown into the harbour.

To be fair, it had been there since 1898 when St Jean had finally embraced the modern world and opened a narrow gauge railway. St Jean was not a place to thrust itself into the limelight; nestling as it did among the reeds and marshes on the Picardie side of the Authie estuary, the town depended on its harbour and the few tourists it could attract. Opening a railway was heady stuff; why, a person could go anywhere they wanted now, even as far as Amiens. In practice, of course, most people were quite content not to go anywhere at all, and the promoters of the railway soon learned that their initial optimism had been cruelly misplaced. However, somehow the railway had survived and business was still as brisk as it had ever been, which is to say not very brisk at all.

Since 1898 then, the engine shed had stood there right on the harbour side minding its own business and no one had given it a second thought; certainly no one had actually spent any money on maintaining it recently, recently being since about the mid nineteen twenties. It had been built of wood, because wood was cheap, but wood does not like standing for sixty years beside a muddy harbour in the face of all the gales coming down La Manche from the North Sea. It doesn't like the long days of mist and drizzle, the hard frosts or even the scorching sun. It was a Swiss cheese of an engine shed; there were holes everywhere, in the walls, in the roof, but as Jacques would tell anyone that mentioned it, they let the smoke from the engines out don't they? It was certainly no good the engine drivers complaining, there was no money spare to fix up the shed, much less build a new one. Life was not easy for a small railway in France in the nineteen fifties, and most of the others around Picardie had closed before the war.....they had only kept going here by a mixture of good luck, good management and turning a blind eye to things like the engine shed.

They couldn't ignore it any longer, though; people tend to notice when an engine shed disappears overnight. You can't just blame the mice or the seagulls like they usually did when things got lost. Jacques was going to have to make that phone call; for the second time that morning, he turned towards his office.

As he sat at his desk, he didn't know what he was going to say. As he dialled the number, he still didn't know. The phone on the other end of the line rang, in the house in Verton of the line superintendent M. Marc Artois, and still Jacques hadn't decided how to begin. The phone was picked up......"Hello?"

"Monsieur Artois, a good morning to you, er.....it is I, Jacques at St Jean sur Mer.... er....we have a small problem here".

"A problem? What sort of a problem is it that gets me out of bed at this hour? Don't tell me the newspapers haven't arrived!".

"No, no, the newspapers have arrived as usual. The problem is that, you see, ...well....the engine shed here at St Jean, it seems to have.....gone".

There was a spluttering noise on the other end of the telephone line.

"Gone? What do you mean, gone? Jacques, what time did you leave the Cafe last night?"

"No, I assure you, I left quite early.......well, fairly early...... No, you see, last night we had an engine shed here, and this morning we haven't. We think the storm in the night has blown it away!"

The phone line had gone quiet; Jacques could hear himself breathing. He wondered if M. Artois was still there. He was; he had been composing himself.

"Are you telling me in all seriousness that the engine shed at your station, the station of which you are in charge, has simply vanished in the night? A whole engine shed, that big wood.............wait a minute! It would have had an engine in it, what's happened to that? You're not telling me that has gone too?"

"No, no, rest assured, the engine is still there on the siding, the number three, she is still there and in one piece. A little damp, but ready to be used today later on when we have brushed the splinters off her and so forth."

"Humph, well that's something; with the Autorail out of action we need all the engines that can turn a wheel. Well, what do you intend to do? It's your station after all".

"Well", Jacques hesitated, "I suppose one of the fishermen might be able to lend us a tarpaulin for a few days, but if this wind keeps on blowing......." he hesitated again." I suppose what we really need is a new engine shed, and quickly".

Jacques was rubbing his ear as he came out of his office and bumped into Louis. M. Artois had not been receptive to the idea of building a new engine shed, and had said so in no uncertain terms! Did Jacques think the railway was made of money, did he think he could just conjure up a new shed out of thin air; really, M. Artois had been quite expressive for a man who had only been awake for five minutes.

"Louis, mon ami, it is not yet seven o'clock in the morning, but I think you and I, we need a Cognac".

As he poured two glasses, Jacques asked "What the hell are we going to do now?".

"I know what I'm not going to do" sniffed Louis, accepting his Cognac, "I'm not preparing my engine in the open air in this weather. Today, yes, but after that you will have to think of something, because I'm not doing it. I'll catch my death of cold, and what's worse the fire-lighting wood is all soaking wet so I can't even get the fire going. If I can't light the fire she won't be ready to take out the 8.30, and what's more you're the one who will have to tell the passengers. Me, I just drive the engine".

This was not turning out to be the best of days.

Warmed by the Cognac, Jacques and Louis walked slowly back to the quayside. The crowds of curious onlookers had begun to disperse - after all, there was nothing to see, all the excitement had happened when it was dark, more's the pity. People began to regard breakfast as more important than staring at the empty space where the shed had been, and they drifted home and to the Cafes to talk about what had happened with friends and family.

Jacques and Louis stood on the harbour wall; the tide had begun to turn, and a few forlorn lengths of splintered timber were now showing above the level of the water. They regarded them much as a man might regard a caterpillar in his salad.

"We can't leave it there". Jacques said, "The fishermen will be up in arms, it's a danger to their boats".

"We'll need a crane to lift them, and a couple of open wagons on the siding at least.....I suppose we can use it for firewood then when it has dried out". Louis was always one for looking on the bright side.

"We can bring the crane wagon from Verton I suppose, that should be strong enough for this....the problem will be getting down there to attach the chain. The damned wood is buried in the mud. Some one is going to have to go down there and......"

"Don't look at me!" Loius looked at Jacques in alarm, "I've got my engine to get ready. In fact, I'm late as it is. Where can I get some dry firewood from?"

As they were talking Louis' fireman, a youth of nineteen called Maurice, came into view walking along the quayside from the town. Maurice wasn't the brightest of lads; he was strong and willing, he would shovel coal all day if you asked him, but as for brains, no, there he was rather lacking. Maurice hadn't noticed that things had changed rather since yesterday; he walked up and stood by the two men. Maurice looked into the green water of the harbour, which was slapping against the increasingly obvious timbers of the engine shed.

"What's that?" he asked?

"That, son, is our engine shed", Louis informed him, taking him by the arm and turning him to face the little locomotive which was now bathed in sunshine.

"It's gone!" cried Maurice. He was a youth of few words. Maurice looked into the water, and again at where the shed had been; the concrete foundations stood out starkly, but standing on them nothing remained. Maurice's brain creaked into action.

"The sheds's gone! Where's the shed gone?" Louis gently took his arm and again indicated the remains in the harbour.

"There, son. That's where the shed's gone. It blew down last night, right into the harbour. What's worse, it's taken our shovels with it, along with half the damn tools and oil cans. But, we've still got an engine to get ready, and if we spend any more time standing here chatting the 8.30 is going to be late and we can't have that. Now, you start oiling round if you can find an oil can still in one piece while I find some dry wood for the fire."

The two of them wandered off, Maurice still looking dazed and Louis determined to show that nothing was going to stop him having his loco ready for the first train of the day.

No3 was still warm, of course; when they put her on shed last night they'd raked out the fire & cleaned the ash pan, but the water in the boiler stayed warm so it wouldn't take long to have her in steam again. Louis glanced at where Jacques was still staring into the harbour, as if mesmerised by the sad remains, and then slipped inside the station building.....Jacques always kept a supply of dry firewood in his office, that would do the job nicely!

Back on the quayside, Jacques was considering his options. He couldn't just pretend that the remains of the engine shed weren't there; at high tide, yes, but now they were displayed for all to see sticking out of the mud. Anyway, it only wanted one damn fool of a fisherman to try and sail over it and that would be that, the cost of a new fishing boat. Even worse, once one had made a claim they'd all be at it, the whole fleet of them, the railway would be bankrupted.

So, how to get rid of it? He could wait for another storm to wash them away, but who knew when that would be? Now the sun was rising higher into a clear blue sky, as though the storm had never been........just when he needed one, there was not a storm to be had.

There was always the crane, of course; fish out the pieces one by one, drop them into a wagon or two, dump them somewhere out of sight when no one was looking. It would take time, and while they were doing it the shed siding would be out of use; they couldn't use the ash pit, or put the engine away in the shed at night.

In the shed - what was he thinking of? It didn't matter where they put the engine at night now! They'd still need to use the pit, though, and the coaling stage. At least the water tower stood by the main line, they could still get to that all right.

As far as he could see, it would have to be the crane; it would be a messy, long laborious job, but the sooner it was started the sooner he could forget about the whole business. Apart from finding a new shed, of course. Jacques set off towards his office and the telephone again; as he went he noticed the first whisps of smoke rising from the funnel of Number 3. Louis must have found some dry firewood from somewhere.

"Hello?".

"Ah, M. Artois, hello, yes, it is me again, Jacques at St Jean sur Mer. I have been thinking about the situation."

"That worries me already! I hope you're going to tell me that it has all been a bad dream?".

"Er, no, it has not unfortunately, it has been all too real. What is left of our engine shed is sitting in the mud of the harbour for all to see now that the tide is dropping, and we will need to remove it, the wood is a danger to the fishing boats. I am requesting the use of the crane wagon from Verton yard, two open wagons and a locomotive of course. It had better be the Locotracteur, a diesel doesn't mind sitting and waiting around as much as a steam engine. I will need some men, of course, say half a dozen, and one of them will have to go down to fit the chain around the pieces of wood. You had better make sure that one of them can swim."

"Is that all? I thought you might be asking for a lot". M. Artois was allowed to be sarcastic, he was the boss.

"That will be all for the moment", Jacques said, "We will get the mess cleared up as quickly as we can. Then there will be the matter of the new shed to consider of course".

For the second time that morning Jacques' ear was in need of some tender loving care.

At least the crane and it's handmaidens should be there by eleven o'clock, it could leave once the 10.30 passenger had reached Verton.

Hah! That gave plenty of time for breakfast; worry made a man hungry. Jacques made for the Cafe Pierre at a steady trot.

****

Somehow, the 8.30 train to Verton got away on time, not that it really mattered because there were no passengers. The nine fifteen from Le Crotoy arrived and was dealt with in the usual manner and for a while it almost seemed as though the day was a perfectly normal one. Jacques sat in his office going though the morning post; outside his window Corpet Louvet No. 4 sizzled and simmered on the middle line, the seagulls screeched and the sun shone. It was all very agreeable.

Until the phone rang. Jacques picked it up absentmindedly, still reading a letter from a farmer who seemed to have received one too few geese the previous Friday.

"Hello, St Jean sur Mer here, how may I help you?".

"It's all right, it's only me", said the telephone as Jacques was jerked back into the present by the voice of M. Artois at Verton. "The crane is on its way, with three open wagons and a Fourgon. I have let you have five men, that is all I can spare, what with the bridge on the Buerk line needing work and the relaying at Rue. You will just have to manage. Oh, and by the way, none of them can swim, so don't go dropping them in the harbour!".

The line went dead.

Sighing, Jacques put on his jacket - one had to look official even when dragging bits of engine shed out of the mud - and walked down to the quayside to wait for the works train. He wasn't intending to do any of the actual work, of course, that was their problem, it was their crane after all, but he had better be here to supervise until more important matters needed his attention, such as lunch. A whistle was carried on the wind from the east, and a couple of minutes later the train clanked over the points and into the station. The Fourgon was uncoupled, and the crane and open wagons were reversed along the quayside and onto the engine shed siding. The driver jumped down from the diesel 'Locotracteur' and lit a cigarette as the five workmen climbed down from the Fourgon and sauntered across to where Jacques was standing.

"Good Morning, Monsieur le Chef, we hear you have lost an engine shed. Very careless, that! I hope you are keeping a close eye on that water tower!" He grinned at his mates.

"Indeed", replied Jacques, "But I am more concerned with getting that lot out of the harbour, which, I am please to say, I can leave in your capable hands. I have important business to attend to. Good day."

Leaving the men to begin preparing the crane, Jacques went back onto the station, pondering the problem of what to do about a new shed. The crews wouldn't put up with working in the open air, not that he blamed them, and it wouldn't do the engines any good in the long run either. On the other hand, there was no money for a replacement, M. Artois had been made himself very clear on that point. So, they must have a new shed, but they couldn't have a new shed, it was as simple as that.

Everyday things occupied him for another hour until the midday train to Le Crotoy had left, and then Jacques decided that lunch could not wait any longer. Walking to the Cafe, he decided to discuss his problem with the fishermen, local businessmen and others who habitually gathered in the Cafe Pierre at this time of day. St Jean almost came to halt between twelve and two; certainly there were no arrivals or departures on the railway, Jacques had seen to that.

Naturally they were waiting for him........there was a barrage of comment as he opened the door, and someone had brought him a dogs lead to tie to the station building so he wouldn't lose that too. It was to be expected, and he put up with it all good naturedly until the right time came to bring a little seriousness into the conversation.

Over his Moules and red wine, Jacques explained his problem; they needed a new engine shed quickly, but they had no money to pay for one. The problem was a simple one, was it not? The solution seemed to be less forthcoming.

"There is an old barn up on Gerard's farm; he might let you have that. Every time one of his cows farts, it leans a little more to the left - it looks just like your old engine shed!"

"No, no, Gerard needs that barn to keep his tractor in, he won't let you have that. Anyway, that old skinflint would charge you more than a new shed would cost".

"Why don't you run the engine back to Verton each night?"

"I'd thought off that one", signed Jacques, "Think of the extra mileage on the loco's, it would wear them out even more than they are worn out already. The drivers and firemen for the morning train all live here, too, how would they get home? They'd never accept it".

Round and round the arguments went, until Jacques' head was spinning. He left them, still coming up with more and more outrageous ideas, and made his way more slowly back to the station. He'd better see how the recovery work was going. As he got near to the crane, another piece of wood was pulled freed from the mud, which gurgled as though it had just been fed and wanted some more. Dripping, the sad remains were swung round and dropped into the wagon, which was filling up fast. Soon they would have to shunt them around so that an empty wagon was next to the crane. The debris in the mud did seem to have shrunk considerably since work began.

"Go and have your lunch; you will have to wait until the 2.05 train has arrived before you can shunt the wagons, anyway. You're doing well".

As Jacques opened his office door, Madame Pinot came in through the door from the street; Madame Pinot did the books, and went round each station in turn on the system. This afternoon being a Thursday it was the turn of St Jean. Jacques didn't much like Thursday afternoons; Madame Pinot could spot a mistake in the book keeping at a hundred metres, and keeping everything neat and orderly was not one of Jacques's strengths. He offered Mme Pinot an absentminded 'Bonjour' and went into his office, where he slumped in the chair and rested his elbows on his desk. What was he going to do?

A moment later, Mme Pinot came in to collect the ledger and the other books, to find him still lost in deep thought.

"Why, M. Rodin, whatever is the matter? You look as though you've lost a train!"

Not living in the town and not having been at work that morning, Mme Pinot was possibly the only person in St Jean that did not know of the loss of the engine shed. Needing no further prompting, Jacques poured out the story, and made as much as he could of his dreadful position as a man caught between a rock and a hard place. He was caught between M. Artois and the engine crews, which was even worse.

"Yes, I understand what you are saying, M. Rodin, but what is the problem?"

"Women!" Thought Jacques to himself, "They can never understand these difficult technical problems which we men have to deal with every day."

He tried to explain again, in words of one syllable. He tried hard not to sigh.

"Yes, Monsieur, I do understand, but I still do not see what the problem is!"

This time Jacques did sigh, he was becoming exasperated with this silly woman wasting his time. "We have no money to replace the engine shed, Madame!" he said very slowly, as to a particularly retarded foreigner. "There is no money!"

"Well, it all seems perfectly simple to me," replied Mme. Pinot briskly, "You pay for a new shed out of the insurance money".

There was a silence. From the colour of his face, Jacques appeared to be struggling for breath.

"Ins.........Ins........" Spluttered Jacques, "Do you mean to tell me that old shed was insured?"

"Of course, the whole railway is insured, public liability for if we damage any of our dear passengers, and cover for Acts of God. It was an Act of God that blew away your engine shed, was it not? Would you like me to telephone the insurance company? They will need to send someone down to see the remains before you take them away."

Mme Pinot was trying not to sound smug, but it was not easy.

"All in good time", Jacques replied, "All in good time. There is someone else who I must telephone first. Would it surprise you to know, Madame Pinot, that our Superintendent of the Line, the admirable, the efficient, the formidable M. Artois is also unaware that we have insurance cover for our missing engine shed? Madame, I shall not take long, but rest assured Madame, I am going to enjoy making this call!".

Chapter 2

THE CRANE

"So, it looks as though you will be getting a new engine shed after all" M. Artois said, "As soon as the insurance money comes through I will let you know, it should pay for a simple structure".

"That is excellent news", Jacques answered, "I will tell Louis, he will be most pleased. Er....did you know that we were insured like that, M. Artois?".

"Of course I knew, it is just that sometimes these things slip ones mind when there is so much important work to be done running the railway. Naturally I knew."

Both men knew that in fact it was Madame Pinot who had known, and had taken great pleasure in informing the pair of them of something of which they should both have been well aware. Both knew, but M. Artois was certainly not going to admit it!

* * * * * * * * * * * * *

Three weeks later, permission had been given for the work to begin. Fortunately, the weather had been fine so Louis and Maurice hadn't grumbled too much about the lack of cover for their locomotive. The concrete foundations of the shed were still in place and undamaged, so they were to be reused; any hopes of something a little larger this time were immediately scuppered when that news leaked out. The new shed would have a steel frame, which could be fixed firmly into the concrete simply by bolting it in place, and the walls would then be built up from concrete blocks. A roof of corrugated sheeting and that would be that, it shouldn't take long to do. At least the new shed should keep the weather out, which is more than the old one ever did within living memory.

Naturally, this being the Cote de Picardie, there was a problem. The steel frames needed to be lifted into position with a crane, and the railway hadn't got one big enough for the job. It looked like a road crane would have to be used, but getting that down to the quayside was not going to be easy. St Jean sur Mer was an old town, with narrow winding streets built long before cars and lorries had been thought of. However, M. Artios had the perfect solution to this problem; "It's your station, Jacques, you sort it out!"

The measurements had been taken, the steel frames sections had been fabricated, and on Wednesday the work was scheduled to begin. It would disrupt the operation of the station, but that couldn't be helped; it shouldn't be for long and at least it would be finished before the Summer season began when trains tended to be longer to cater for the tourists. A crane had been hired and was expected first thing in the morning. Jacques was at the station bright and early, not so much because he was needed to do anything but because he was simply excited and didn't want to miss it. Anyway, it was his station, he would be expected to be there; he had put on his best uniform in honour of the occasion.

Eight o'clock came and went.........quarter past.........half past. The men who were to erect the shed had arrived and were milling about on the quayside; all the materials had arrived the previous day on a train of open wagons and were standing ready on the quayside siding. All that was needed was the crane.

Louis the engine driver came into the station building to sign in for duty; his engine was not here today as it would have been in the way of the work, Verton would be supplying one instead so he had nothing to prepare but he still had to show that he had been at work if required.

"Have you heard about the crane?" he asked Jacques? "It's stuck in the Rue des Moulins".

"What!" Cried Jacques, "Stuck? Stuck where?"

"Stuck next to the shop of M. Philipe and the Cafe, it's blocking the whole road. I was there when it happened, just passing; the end of the crane went straight through the window above the Cafe.......there was such a scream! Then young Marianne put her head out of the window - I swear to you, Jacques, you would not think she is only sixteen! - to see what was going on. When she leaned right out to swear at the crane driver, I nearly fell off my bike! She may look like an angel but she swears like a fisherman, I don't think she repeated herself once." Louis chuckled at the memory.

Jacques waited to hear no more, throwing on his jacket he rushed out of the door and headed up the station approach road towards the old part of town. "You sort it out!" he had been told. No one had thought to tell him how.

The crane was jammed where the narrow road made a tight bend and the buildings on each side overhung; the cab was on the pavement blocking the door to the Boulangerie of M. Phillipe, and the end of the jib was sticking through the upstairs window of the Cafe where a white lace curtain had wrapped itself around the pulley wheel. The crane couldn't go forwards, and it couldn't go backwards either. 'Stuck' about summed it up.

When Jacques arrived he had to push his way through the usual crowd of onlookers that gathers whenever something goes wrong. The crane diver was arguing with M. Philipe, who was leaning out of the window of his shop due to front bumper of the crane being right in the doorway. He seemed less than impressed when the driver shrugged and said that there was nothing he could do, and when Jacques asked what they were going to do he had to endure a torrent of pent up emotion from both men. Two gendarmes stood a little further up the street watching, but they did not offer any suggestions and after five minutes they went back up the hill to direct any traffic round the top of the town and away from the blockage.

"Well", Jacques said when they finally had to pause for breath, "One thing is for sure, it can't stay here. I don't think we can try and get any further down the street towards the quay, but if it got this far it should be possible to reverse back out again. Don't worry about any damage, M. Philipe, it will be covered by the insurance!". M. Philipe couldn't see that his fingers were crossed behind his back............Jacques wasn't at all sure that this counted as an 'Act of God'.

It took them an hour, but finally they dislodged the jib of the crane from the Cafe window, and with the lace curtain still attached and flapping in the breeze the crane was backed carefully along the street whence it had come. Jacques walked in front of it, feeling hot and conspicuous in his uniform yet not wanting to trust anyone else to get the crane to where it was needed. He'd already had to promise Madame Charles at the Cafe a new window and a complete set of curtains for her upstairs rooms, and heaven knew who was going to pay for that. The Boulangerie thankfully had not been damaged, other than the pride of M. Philipe of course, and that would sooth itself in due course even if it did cost Jacques a few glasses of wine.

* * * * * * * * * * * * *

Once the crane had reached the top of the Rue des Moulins, it could at last be backed into the yard of the Ecole and turned to face the way it needed to go. There was no way, seemingly, of getting it to the quayside by road, but Jacques had an idea. If the crane was needed on the railway, why not drive it along the railway? The line being narrow gauge the crane's wheels should straddle the rails and be able to run along the sleepers at either side; at least it was worth a try. Jacques stood on the step of the cab, and words were exchanged with the driver. After a few minutes, Jacques climbed into the cab and directed the crane out of the town and across the bridge spanning a small stream that ran into the Authie. A kilometre beyond that the road crossed the railway on the level and it should be possible to get onto the line there.

It was now half past ten; the passenger train to Le Crotoy would have gone, no freight was running because of the work on the shed, and the Verton train wasn't due until nearly twelve o'clock. They would have time!

The crane drove onto the level crossing, and with Jacques now standing in front it swung off the road onto the railway track. The wide tyres of the crane fitted nicely on either side of the rails, and at a very reduced speed it began to proceed along the tracks at a slow pace with Jacques walking in front. He wasn't enjoying this; he would not be happy until the crane was safely at the station and he could go and recover in his office.

The crane scrunched over the ballast, and Jacques tried not to think about what the heavy vehicle was doing to the ends of the sleepers, most of which weren't in the first flush of youth. They made progress until they came to the trestle bridge over the same stream that they had crossed on the road. The trestle was wooden, it was two hundred metres long, and the tracks on it were not laid on sleepers but on long timbers parallel with the rails. Jacques stopped. The crane stopped. Jacques took off his uniform cap and scratched his head. The driver leaned out of his cab and asked what they were going to do now.

"We will proceed!" Jacques called to him, and continued to walk towards the bridge. The crane followed.

On either side of the rails the bridge was planked, mainly as a walkway for men working on the track and as a right of way for fishermen and the like. The crane should be able to run along the planked pathway and off the other end of the bridge with no difficulty. The front wheels of the crane, watched carefully by Jacques, slowly passed from the ballast and sleepers onto the bridge. It was unfortunate that the planking was lower then the normal track due to the timber baulks carrying the rails, and as it moved forwards the crane's front axle was resting on the rails with the wheels a good ten centimetres above the level of the planks. Equally unfortunately the crane was driven from the back axle, which continued to push the vehicle along with the front axle sliding on the rails until the rear axle too passed onto the bridge at which point the rear wheels, carried forwards by the momentum of the crane, also began to spin uselessly in mid air.

The crane was stranded; nothing the driver did made any difference; with all four wheels off the ground it was suspended by its axles, and it wasn't going anywhere.

"Very enterprising, this plan of yours," commented the driver after he had climbed down, kicked a tyre, spat into the river and then settled on the side of the bridge with his arms folded.

"This wasn't my idea", his body language shouted. "It's nothing to do with me".

"What are we going to do now?" Jacques appealed. "The train from Verton will be here soon, we can't leave the line blocked like this!"

Of course, leave the line blocked was exactly what they did have to do. Jacques ran back down the track to the level crossing, grabbed a red flag from the crossing keeper and flagged down the Verton train a hundred metres from the crossing. Once all had been explained, the locomotive was uncoupled and drew forwards until it was behind the crane. Happily the crane was well equipped with stout ropes, and one could be hung over the coupling hook and attached to the rear of the crane. The crane driver got back aboard, and the locomotive gently pulled the stricken vehicle backwards until the rear wheels could get a grip on solid ground. Jacques unhooked the rope, the loco whistled triumphantly and backed onto its train while the crane trundled off the bridge, very carefully. Once back at the level crossing, it turned onto the road and headed away without another word and nothing more was seen of it that day.

Jacques wearily climbed into the Fourgon with the guard of the train, and they set off at reduced speed over the trestle and into St Jean station. The passengers all had their heads out of the coach windows; nothing this exciting had happened for years! Wait until they could tell all their friends about it in the town!

Jacques knew one thing; he had better tell Verton what had happened before word got back to them any other way. He trudged towards his office, hot, sweaty and fed up; there was no sign of the men who should have been building the shed. Probably given up and gone to the Cafe, he thought. I wish I was with them.

The phone call to Verton was not pleasant; M. Artois was coming down straight away. There would have to be a speed limit put on the trestle until it could be checked for damage, likewise the length of track from the crossing, and the men who were meant to be building the shed should be sent back to Verton by the next train where they could be found something useful to do. The railway was not designed for the use of heavy road vehicles, and M. Artois was amazed that Jacques had thought such a hair brained scheme would work. They were lucky there had not been more disruption to traffic..........M. Artois expressed himself at considerable length and left no doubt about who he blamed for the whole situation.

Jacques waited in his office; he couldn't face lunch.

In the end, the crane was driven onto the loading bank at Verton station and from there onto a flat wagon which then proceeded with the Locotracteur and a Fourgon to St Jean sur Mer. There the procedure was reversed and the crane was able to drive off the loading bank and across the tracks to the site of the shed to do its work as planned. It finished in less than a day.......oddly enough, the crane had a different driver this time.

Eight broken sleepers needed replacing between the crossing and the bridge, but that length of track was getting near the end of its life anyway so it just hastened what was already planned.

The Cafe window had been replaced and Madame Charles had spent a very enjoyable day in Amiens choosing some very expensive new curtains for her bedrooms.....in the end, the railway had paid for the work and Jacques heard no more about it from Verton. He heard a lot more about it from his friends in St Jean, though, so much so that he almost stopped going to the Cafe until his natural good humour re-established itself. Merde, what a time it had been. A nice quiet life was all he wanted, and what did he get? Problem after problem! Jacques poured himself another strong cup of coffee and sat watching the sun glinting on the water of harbour from his office window.

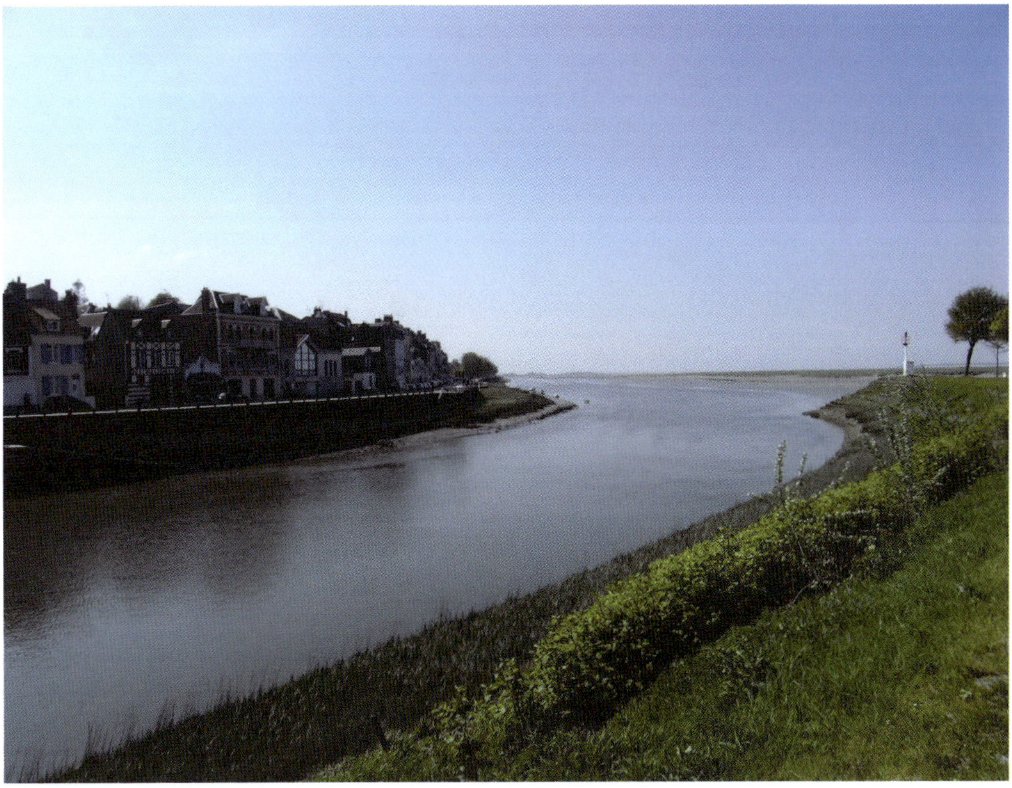

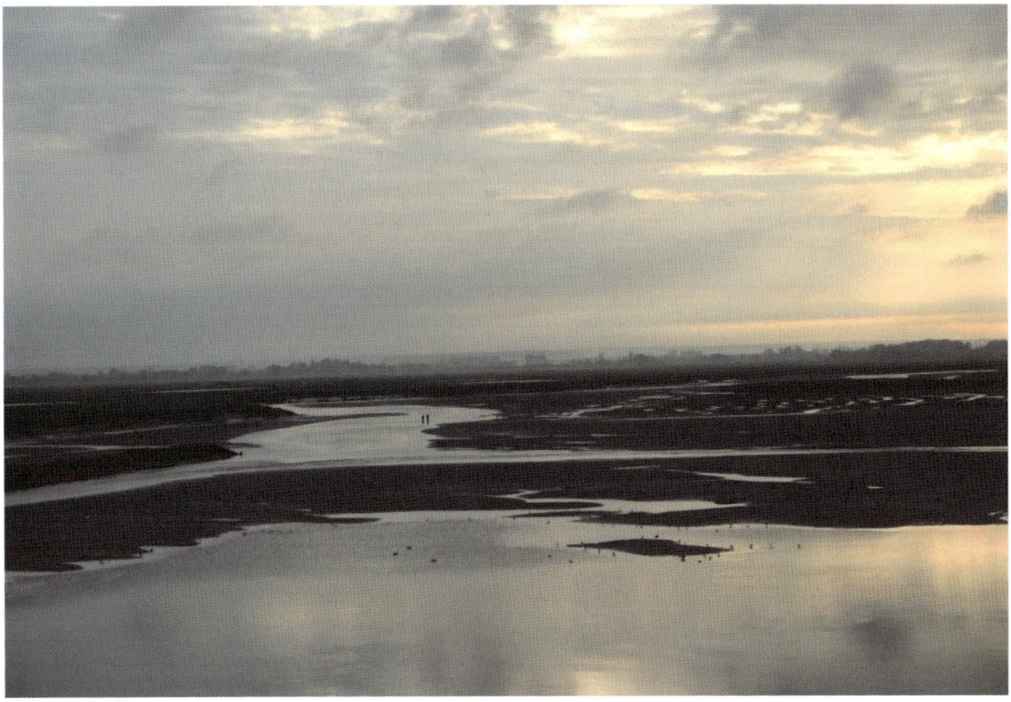

Chapter 3

SOMETHING IN THE MUD

The estuary of the river Authie was beautiful at full tide, but even its most ardent admirers would have to admit that at low tide the exposed banks of mud were rather less appealing, both to look at and to inhale. The harbour at St Jean sur Mer had a substantial stone wall along the quayside but on the opposite bank of the river the mud banks reigned supreme until the coast itself was reached where sandy beaches were to be found…that was a kilometre beyond the town, however. When the tide was out the harbour was of limited use, with most of the boats beached on the mud until the waters rose again. Coastal traffic had pretty much ceased to exist, the port relying on the fishing boats for its income these days. At one time the little station had been busy loading and unloading cargo for the vessels that sailed up and down the coast, but now the sidings were quiet and boxes of fish were the only significant traffic carried on the railway from the quay.

Jacques liked to walk along the quayside, breathing in the sea air and taking in the busy scene as the fishing boats went about their business. His station included this section of the quay, though he shared responsibility for it with the Harbour Master. This Monday morning he wasn't inclined to linger; it was a bit drizzly and as the tide was out the area was a bit aromatic. He hurried along past the bollards until something caught his eye sticking out of the mud. He stopped to have a closer look; the object was cylindrical, with fins at the end that was sticking out of the mud. It was black, shiny in the wet atmosphere. Jacques gulped; it wasn't possible was it? Could it be what it looked like; was he standing three metres away from an unexploded bomb?

He looked around – there was no one else to be seen, the weather was keeping everyone indoors. On shaking legs he hurried up to the station; he needed to telephone the Gendarmarie.

Half an hour later a Police car pulled up outside the station and an officer that Jacques didn't know got out; he came across to the station, and Jacques lead him onto the quayside to where he had seen the bomb. The scene there had changed however; in the meantime the tide had turned and the place where the bomb had been was now under water. There was nothing to be seen. Jacques felt stupid, but he knew what he had seen and he was worried about it. St Jean had mercifully escaped any serious damage during the war, but a stray aircraft jettisoning its bomb load was certainly not unheard of and they could have landed anywhere.

There was nothing for it but to wait for low tide again and hope the thing was still there; the Gendarme arranged to come back that evening, and left Jacques to get on with the business of running the station. He didn't say anything to anyone, there was no point worrying the staff, but he found it difficult to settle to anything himself. By mid afternoon he was a bag of nerves and he was relieved to see the Police car drive up to the station shortly after the last train had departed.

Again he lead the officer across the station to the quayside, and this time when they looked over the wall the mud banks were uncovered and the black object was one more in clear view.

"Merde!" said the Gendarme. "You were right!"

"I was hoping it would have gone" admitted Jacques, but there it was, there was no escaping it. It looked like a bomb.

The Gendarme needed to consult a superior officer; the superior officer needed to consult someone even more superior and that exalted gentleman then called the army. By that time it was getting dark, and the tide was coming in again. There was nothing to be done until the following morning. The gendarme went home and Jacques went to the Cafe….he needed a drink.

The following morning the sun was shining and the weather looked to be set fair. By the time Jacques got to the station the quayside was already an animated scene, with soldiers and Police peering over the wall into the mud and water below. An area had been roped off, and more Police were patrolling it to keep onlookers away. Jacques went across to introduce himself but he was told quite firmly that he was not required and that he should remain in the station with all the windows open in case there was a blast. Looking out from his office he could see a man donning a wet suit and a few minutes later he was being lowered over the edge of the quayside on a rope.

It was a quiet scene; all the fishing boats had been moved away to other moorings and there was none of the usual hustle and bustle of a working harbour and station. Jacques wasn't sure what they intended to do about the first train when it was due; he'd give it ten minutes and then go and ask them. He busied himself tidying the station building until he was disturbed by a knock on the door; it was the Gendarme he had seen yesterday.

"Good morning Monsieur", the officer said. "I am pleased to report that there is no cause for alarm, the item in the mud turned out to be a fishing float of an unusual design. I must admit that it fooled me, and I must emphasise that you did exactly the right thing in reporting it. Well, good morning, Monsieur, and next time you find a bomb, call someone else!"

With that he left, and the others appeared to be doing the same; within five minutes the quayside was deserted. That solved the problem of the first train. Jacques was relieved that he hadn't mentioned the bomb to anyone; hopefully no one would ever hear about it.

He went outside to welcome the first train of the day from Verton; as it pulled into the station it slowed down; unseen by Jacques the fireman had jumped down from the engine, run ahead and put a detonator on the rail. As the locomotive ran over it the detonator exploded with a loud 'crack', and Jacques knew at once that his secret was out; every window on the train had a grinning face at it, and the loco crew were lying on the ground holding their sides, they were laughing so much that they couldn't stand. Jacques went back inside; Madame Artur could collect the tickets today.

Things were quiet then until lunch time when Jacques went to the Café Pierre; they had gone to lot of trouble, he had to admit. When he opened the door the string fuse on a large round black bomb standing on a table began to fizz, and everyone in the Café shouted 'Boom'! The place was packed, it looked as if the whole damn town was there. There was nothing to be done but grin and bear it, and at least they did offer to buy him a drink. He needed it.

Back at the station he hid in his office until late in the afternoon, when the phone rang. It was M. Artois from Verton.

"Hello Jacques, I've been hearing about your bomb!" he began.

"Everyone seems to have heard about my bomb" groaned Jacques.

"They would have done if it had gone off "M. Artos went on. "Seriously, Jacques, you did exactly the right thing. If that had been a bomb and it had exploded it would have taken out half the town and your station would have ceased to exist. I want to commend you, your alertness could have saved a very nasty situation."

M. Artois rang off and Jacques sat back in his chair; to be praised by M. Artois was a rare enough event for it to need savouring at length. Perhaps he would go the Café again that evening after all.

Chapter 4

THE AUTORAIL

The phone call had been quite explicit; that diesel railcar had cost a lot of money, and you're not using it enough. The passengers like it, it is cheap to run and the SNCF at Verton don't laugh at us so much when we use it, so get used to the idea because it is here to stay.

The railcar was new; they'd only had it for a few days, and it was the pride of the management up in Verton.

Jacques couldn't really complain; he'd been avoiding using the damn thing wherever possible and putting a steam train on instead, using any excuse he could think of. He liked steam locomotives, that was all there was to it. This big gaudy red and cream Autorail just wasn't the same, it didn't sound right, or smell right; it didn't even look like a train. A train should have an engine at the front with coaches behind, or a mixture of coaches and wagons in the case of most of the trains on the Cote de Picardie. The railcar was new, efficient, cheap, it had padded seats in place of the wooden slats in the other coaches, and it didn't need turning after a journey, the driver just walked to the other end and off he went in the other direction. You couldn't argue against it, the railcar was the future and using it could make the difference between the company surviving or going to the wall.

Nevertheless, Jacques hated it. He was responsible for the smooth running of St Jean station and he had to keep his customers happy, and that included the fishermen; what the management at Verton didn't realise was that there was no where on the railcar to put the boxes of shellfish which needed to get to the SNCF as quickly as possible. It was all right at the moment when most of the trains were still steam hauled, but what of the future? The blasted thing filled his office with diesel fumes too so that he had to keep the window shut, and most worrying of all if it was a success and they bought more of them, what would happen to the steam locomotives then? It was very worrying.

When the first train from Verton arrived at St Jean sur Mer on that Monday morning in May, it was the Autorail that rumbled over the trestle bridge, past the water tower and into the station. It had a good load of passengers on board, having connected with the Paris express, and it did look colourful standing there in the sunshine on the middle road. Jacques looked out of the window of his office at the bustling scene, trying not to accept that what he was looking at was the way the railway needed to go. He might love steam engines, but then he didn't have to prepare, fire & drive them, let alone clean them, while the passengers didn't seem to be missing the smuts on their clothes and the cinders in their hair. He grunted to himself; this modern contraption might look all very well, but it wasn't flexible enough. What would happen in a month or so when the tourist season was upon them and the passenger numbers often trebled; what then?

The trouble was, the boss only looked at the figures, and the figures were telling him that the Autorail saved money. What else could possibly matter when money was being saved?

Not until he was walking back from the Cafe Pierre after lunch did Jacques have an idea of how he might make his point, without actually being seen to do so. As the afternoon wore on he became more and more convinced that it would work.

The following day, the Autorail again came in on the morning train, but Jacques hardly gave it a second glance. Once all the tickets had been checked, he went down to the quayside where several fishing boats were tied up. Most of the fishing from St Jean was for shellfish from the estuary and along the shore to the north and south; the crabs and lobsters caught there were famous and much prized in top Paris restaurants. They had to get to Paris while they were fresh, of course, in fact they were sent live in boxes filled with ice. Normally, they travelled in the 'Fourgon', the brake van which also took small goods, parcels and the like. The guards were used to the smell of the fish, and they knew that now and again a big lobster or crab would come their way.

Jacques wanted something specific from the fishermen, and they were happy to oblige him as an old friend who could be relied on to buy the wine that evening in the Cafe. Half an hour before the 3pm train to Verton was due to leave, a large pile of fish boxes appeared by the side of the track in the station, labelled 'Urgent, to go by the next available train'.

Well, the next available train was the Autorail, so the porter did as he was bid and loaded the boxes, stacking them in the space between the doors. It was a hot, humid afternoon, and the Autorail was well loaded with shoppers and tourists travelling back to Verton. Promptly at three o'clock the horn hooted and the Autorail grunted and clanked its way over the points and out of the station. Jacques watched it go, and grinned. Those boxes, so considerately placed there by the fishermen were full of fish that normally would have been thrown over the side as unsellable, and somehow they seemed to have forgotten to put in any ice.

The Autorail was hot and stuffy; the only openings were small sections at the top of the windows which slid open a few centimetres but they didn't help much at all. The driver at the front was OK, he had a proper opening window next to him, but everyone else was stuck inside on this humid afternoon with six boxes of fragrant fish, and the fragrance was making itself known to everyone on board. The poor guard took the brunt of the complaints, but all he could do was point to the label which said that the boxes must travel without fail by the next train. Oddly enough, when he read it more closely, there was no mention of what was to happen to them when they arrived at Verton, that section seemed to have been left blank for some reason. Most strange.

Be that as it may, on the journey across the marshes and fields of western Picardie the railcar became a most unpleasant place to be. The boxes had begun to leak water onto the floor, and as the railcar leaned into the bends the stream of water flowed first one way, then the other around the feet of the poor passengers. People gasped for air, people choked, people moved as far away as they could get from those boxes, but it didn't help - there was no escape from the stench.

By the time they reached Verton some passengers were green, some were white, and all were angry. As one person they made for the office of M. Artois, the superintendent of the line. Unfortunately for M. Artois, he was in his office and had not time to escape before the door flew open and a dozen voices at once demanded to know what he intended to do.

The telephone in the office of the Chef de Gare at St Jean sur Mer rang shortly before four o'clock, as Jacques had known that it would. He had been depending on it, in fact.

"What the hell were those boxes of fish doing on the Autorail?" Shouted M. Artois as soon as the phone was picked up. "I've had a train load of very upset passengers here; who authorised putting that fish on the train?".

"Good afternoon, M. Artois", answered Jacques calmly - he knew that would infuriate the Superintendent even more. "Why, I authorised it. We always send our boxes of fish to you by passenger train, it is the quickest way. We normally put them in the Fourgon, of course, as they can get a bit smelly, but the Autorail does not have a Fourgon, does it? How else was I to get them away from here this afternoon?"

It took twenty minutes to make M. Artois appreciate that the traffic in fish from St Jean actually made more money for the railway than the passengers other than in the height of the tourist season, and if all the passenger trains were going to be diesel railcars in the future, well, Jacques really couldn't see any other way of doing it. The fish couldn't travel by the goods trains, they were too slow what with needing to shunt at every station and the fish must without fail meet the main line trains to Paris.

M. Artois knew all this perfectly well, of course, but he wasn't thinking very straight just at the moment.

It was then that Jacques dropped in the line he had been leading up to all this time.

"Perhaps if it is not possible to carry the fish in the railcar, we will need to replace it with a steam train again."

When M. Artois put down the phone, Jacques thought that he had made a good case for reinstating steam on all the passenger trains, as only a steam engine pulled a Fourgon for carrying the fish. What could be simpler? That evening in the Cafe, Jacques bought wine for the fishermen with a good grace, for without them he might still be stuck with that horrible diesel thing. He wondered which of the steam engines Verton would put on the first train in the morning?

Jacques was at the station bright and early on Wednesday morning to see the first train of the day arrive; he was looking for traces of smoke in the distance. Nothing could be seen yet, but no matter, Verton were sure to have put on a steam train this morning. He had made sure that there was a consignment of shellfish - a real consignment this time- that needed to be transported to Paris forthwith.

Imagine his surprise, then, when a whistle sounded as the train approached the trestle bridge - not a steam whistle, but the deeper tones of the Autorail's horn. Bu that was impossible, surely Verton knew about the fish waiting to go out?

Verton knew all right; when the Autorail pulled into the station, trailing behind it was a covered van ready to be loaded with as much fish as was necessary. The works at Verton had performed miracles - and worked late onto the night on overtime - fitting couplings to the railcar so that it could pull a van behind it. The speed was reduced a little and the radiator was overheating rather, but it had solved the problem of what to do about the fish. Once the passengers had disappeared into the station building, the Autorail was uncoupled and ran round the loop line so that the van was on the other end, and there it was ready to leave for Verton with people and fish firmly separated.

As Jacques slumped in his chair in his office, the phone rang.

"I wanted to thank you, Jacques, for your helpful comments about the Autorail", said M. Artois smugly, "As you can see, we have solved the problem. I am having a purpose built trailer made for it, but the van will do for the time being. I think now we can go ahead and order another Autorail for the Le Crotoy line, what do you think?".

Jacques didn't know what to think. He'd been out manoeuvred. No wonder M. Artois was the boss, the cunning devil.

Chapter 5

DERAILMENT

A low mist hung over the harbour at St Jean sur Mer as Jacques unlocked the door of the station building, promising another fine day. That was good news for the railway; the fine weather brought in the tourists and there was the prospect of the line actually making some money for a change. It was Saturday morning and the town was coming slowly to life; the pace of life in St Jean didn't encourage rushing about at this early hour. The first train wasn't due to arrive at St Jean for fifty minutes yet but Jacques liked to have time to make sure everything was in order. It was also the only time of day when he had the station to himself, which he rather enjoyed. He pottered around, humming to himself contentedly.

The whistle of the train for the crossing a kilometre from the station brought him out onto the front of the station. Normally the Autorail was used for the early train but on a Summer Saturday they reverted to a steam loco with three coaches in anticipation of more passengers than the Autorail could comfortably handle. Jacques listened to the train as it approached the station; was it his imagination or did it sound different? There was something about the tone of the whistle and the exhaust beat as the loco ran over the trestle bridge and along the embankment alongside the estuary…..he could see the smoke now. As the train came into view, jolting over the points by the loco shed, Jacques took a couple of paces closer – it was a steam loco, but it wasn't one he'd seen before. All the Cote de Picardie loco's were painted a dark Burgundy red but this one was a bright green. It was larger too, it had an extra set of carrying wheels under the smokebox and a much longer boiler. Where could it have come from?

As the train drew to a halt Jacques walked alongside it; he had his duties to perform but once the last ticket had been collected he walked across to the loco which had uncoupled and was standing at the end of the station on the headshunt. One of the Verton drivers was in the cab; as Jacques approached the loco gave a toot on the whistle and ran smartly back along the outside track in order to run round the three coaches. The fireman, who had climbed down to change the points, trotted after it leaving Jacques standing alone scratching his head. He walked slowly back towards the station, wishing he hadn't put on his heavy uniform jacket. As he did so there was a shout from the end of the station, a grinding noise and a sound of escaping steam. Jacques couldn't see what was going on, the coaches were in the way, but whatever it was it didn't sound good. He began to run along the side of the train and as he did so other people with the same idea joined him – it was amazing how an empty station could suddenly attract a crowd as soon as something unusual happened. Reaching the end of the coaches he stopped; now he could see what had caused the grinding noise. The locomotive was resting across the point by the water tank at an angle with all six driving wheels off the track, the rear wheels in the ballast and the crew standing alongside it looking as though they wished they were somewhere else. The point on which they had derailed was the one leading into the station over which every train arriving or leaving had to pass; St Jean sur Mer station was effectively blocked, nothing could get in or out.

Panting, Jacques ran along the track; the St Jean driver and fireman, Louis & Maurice had arrived too after coming to prepare their engine for the first rain to Le Crotoy. The three of them reached the derailed loco at the same time, which meant there were now five people standing looking at it not knowing what the hell to do. The driver from Verton, who Jacques now recognised as Claude Dubois, took off his cap to wipe some sweat from his brow; the mist was clearing and the day was getting hotter by the minute.

"Where did you find this thing?" asked Jacques. "I've never seen it before". Looking up at it from track level the locomotive towered over them, with tall side tanks and a large boiler. If it hadn't been straddling the point as it was it would have looked most impressive.

"They've just bought two of them" Claude told him, "They came from up Calais way, they were going for scrap so we got them for next to nothing. They are powerful engines, we thought they'd pull longer trains and perhaps use less coal. Unfortunately they are also a good bit bigger than our little Corpet's and with our track the way it is maybe they are too big and heavy. We nearly came off before we got out of the yard at Verton, and she was rolling a bit coming along beside the river. It was only a matter of time before this happened."

"Well, we've got to get it moved" Jacques said, "It's blocking the whole station".

"And how do you suggest we do that?" asked Claude.

Of course, that was the problem. The loco carried a jack but that was for minor derailments, a single wheel coming off the track, not for something like this.

"I'll go and ring Verton" Jacques said and began the long walk back to the station building. They would have to suspend all the trains for the moment, with the loco where it was the lines to Verton and Le Crotoy were both affected. The whole Cote de Picardie system was shut down; it couldn't have happened in a worse place.

Once they had word of the derailment at Verton things moved quickly; the Locotracteur was dispatched with a crew of men in a Fourgon and the crane truck. When it arrived half an hour later there was another problem; the Locotracteur and the Fourgon were between the crane and the derailed locomotive which was not a lot of use so the whole lot had to run back up the line to the loop at Rue where the crane could be put on the front and propelled back to St Jean. By the time it arrived the station was buzzing with people; something like this always brought out the crowds, eager to watch what was happening and safe in the knowledge that it wasn't their problem. The men from Verton jacked up the derailed locomotive and bit by bit with the help of the crane began to swing it round so that it was facing the right way again. They got the front driving wheels onto the track, then gently pulled it backwards until it was clear of the damaged point before lowering the other wheels into place. The loco didn't seem to be damaged and of course it was still in steam so Claude had orders to return it to Verton light engine....very slowly and carefully....so that it could be properly inspected in the workshop. The breakdown train was in the way of course, so that had to run back to Rue so the green loco could pass it in the loop after which it came back to St Jean to see what else was required before the line could be reopened.

There were two problems; a train standing in St Jean station with no locomotive to pull it, and the damaged point leading into the station over which all the traffic had to pass. When the breakdown train returned Jacques walked up to it and stood alongside the foreman from Verton. Six sleepers were smashed, the rail was bent and one of the point blades had been separated from the tie bar. It was a mess.

This was going to take time; new parts would have to be fetched from Verton and then fitted which could take most of the day. The breakdown train headed north again and Jacques went back to the station to report of what had happened to M. Artois. He put a big notice on the door of the station saying that services were suspended and giving the times of the buses to Verton and Le Crotoy. That was the hardest thing of all, but there was no alternative. With no tickets to sell or passengers to deal with he went into the office and made a cup of coffee; he had sent Madame Artur home, there was nothing for her to do at the station. Louis & Maurice were using the time to give their engine a good clean, something that most days there wasn't the time to do.

The track gang arrived back at just after eleven o'clock; Verton had decided that the simplest thing to do was take out the whole point and replace it with a new one. The track at St Jean has been in place since the line had opened in 1898....most of it was buried in granite setts to give a flat surface on the quayside so maintenance had been confined to looking at the bits that were actually visible and hoping for the best where the rest was concerned. Speeds were low in the station so it wasn't too much of an issue, until someone had the bright idea of using large heavy locomotives of course. Looking on the bright side, the smashed point was beyond the quayside so it could be got at easily enough; it was just a case of removing the bolts in the fishplates and lifting it out, then hoping that the replacement would fit without too much trouble. Verton always kept some spares at the works for occasions like this and a narrow gauge point fitted nicely onto a flat wagon in one piece. The old ballast was scraped away and the new point lowered into place with the crane, the adjacent rails needing a little tweaking until everything fitted snugly together and the fishplates could be replaced. The adjacent hand lever was connected to the tie bar and all was well; by three o'clock the job was complete and the new point was ready to be used. The timetable was all over the place by now of course so it was decided that the best thing to do was simply wait until the following morning and start again then. The Locotracteur trundled back to Verton with the works train, after which Louis & Maurice could take back the three empty coaches ready for the morning train tomorrow. It was a Sunday and normally there wouldn't be a lot happening but in the tourist season the passenger timetable was used seven days a week.

Jacques used the time to have a look at the new point; it stood out like a sore thumb, the rails rusty as no traffic had yet run over it. It seemed to have fitted in place OK at least, give it a few days and no one would know anything had happened. Jacques was more concerned about the rest of the station now, with the pointwork that hadn't been renewed….if these new engines were going to be used regularly it was only a matter of time before the same thing happened again. If he was honest none of the trackwork was in good condition, and some of the points were frankly deplorable but they had always got away with it, the little Corpet Louvet tanks just bounced over the rough bits and carried on going. One thing was certain, the railway certainly couldn't afford to replace them all, and no doubt the other stations on the system were just as bad.

On Monday morning word came back to him from Verton that it had been decided to confine the two now locomotives to the Verton to Berck section; the track on that line had been renewed in the 1930's so it was practically brand new!

Chapter 6

ROAST DUCK

There was a deferential knock on the office door. Madame Pinot put her head round, and said "I thought you might like to know that M. Artois has just got off the train from Verton".

Jacques dropped his pen on the floor. "What, here? Now? Why?".

"I am not a mind reader, M. Rodin, I do not know why. However, if you wait a moment you will be able to ask him yourself, because he is coming this way". Mme. Pinot closed the door behind her, greeting M. Artois as he came into the station building. She had known him for years, since when he had been just a ticket clerk at Berck station and she had been a regular passenger to and from school. Unlike Jacques, she was not afraid of him, in fact she rather liked him.

"Bonjour Yvette, it is nice to see you", M. Artois boomed. He tended to project his voice like a buffalo on the great plains, even when there were only the two of them present. He was the only person on the staff of the Cote de Picardie that dared to call Madame Pinot by her Christian name, too........certainly Jacques would never have taken the risk. M. Artois, unlike Jacques, suited his position in the hierarchy of the railway; he was a large imposing man who looked as though he would complement a dress uniform or a Mayoral chain, which, as he was also the Mayor of Verton, was a very good thing.

"Is he in the office? I need a word, we've had a complaint. Normally I wouldn't bother, but this was from Monsieur le Docteur Claude so I have to be seen to be doing something."

M. Artois knocked briefly and opened the office door; Jacques was waiting to greet him and offer him the only comfortable chair. "This is a pleasure, Monsieur", Jacques lied. "What brings you to St Jean this afternoon?".

"I've had a complaint from one of the regular passengers on the afternoon train from Le Crotoy, Jacques, one of the passengers that I cannot just ignore. It seems that the train always stops at the level crossing just beyond Rue, even when there is no road traffic, and Old George the crossing keeper passes something up into the cab of the engine while some lumps of coal accidentally fall from the bunker. George has his coal allowance, and if that is being supplemented from the engines it has got to stop".

"Of course", Jacques "That will certainly be the best plan. Louis and Maurice are on that train this week. Would you like me to come with you? I would hate you to get that nice coat dirty on the footplate. Perhaps you would like me to go instead?"

"That will not be necessary!" barked M.Artois, and he left the office to wait outside for the train. Jacques remained in his office, frantically trying to think of a way to warn Louis to get rid of those ducks, but nothing came to mind, it was too late. The train was almost here, in fact at that moment he heard it whistle for the footpath which crossed the line half a kilometre from the station. Jacques put on his jacket and went outside to await the inevitable. He just hoped that Francois the Butcher wouldn't come down to pay for his ducks just yet, that would make things even worse.

He stood just behind M. Artois as the train approached, the elderly Corpet Lovet tank engine lurching over the point by the water tower and onto the middle road. The brakes squealed as it drew to a halt, and the passengers began to disembark. M. Artois walked purposefully towards the engine. At the same moment, Louis at last looked around the side of the cab.......Jacques was signalling frantically to him, but there was no need, Louis wasn't slow on the uptake. As M. Artois reached the engine, Louis leaned over the side and made a great show of surprise and delight at seeing his distinguished visitor. M. Artois climbed up into the cab.

"Louis, I want to check that there is nothing here that shouldn't be here". He began opening the toolboxes, but there was nothing in those except tools; beyond that, frankly, there was not much else to examine, as the cab on a Corpet Louvet is not commodious and has few places where anything could be hidden. Louis was the picture of innocence, Maurice had been sent to oil the valve gear on the other side of the engine and now Jacques was standing there looking up at them, his expression a mixture of relief and puzzlement. M. Artois grunted and climbed down.

"Well, Louis, it seems as though I need not have troubled you. I will have a word with the coal man at Le Crotoy, though; it seems as though he has perhaps been giving you too much if pieces are falling off the engine. Especially around Rue. You follow my meaning?".

M. Artois stalked off, and Jacques hurried to follow him. As they did so, M. Artois suddenly stopped dead in his tracks. He sniffed. Yes, there was no doubt about it, a delicious smell of roast duck was wafting across the station. He looked towards the Cafe, but there no sign of any-one there. Most odd. M. Artois went into the station; he might as well have a look at the books while he was here.

"You'd better get rid of them" Jacques advised, "I wouldn't put it past him to come back for another look. I think our little arrangement had better be put on hold for a while; you'd better tell Georges what has happened. I will pop up to the Boulangerie later on. It's a shame, it was working so well, but all good things come to an end."

With that, Jacques left Louis to uncouple the coaches and went back inside; the smell of roast duck was making him feel hungry.

Chapter 7

MADAME PINOT

It was Thursday. On Thursday afternoons Madame Pinot came to St Jean station to do the books for the week and to correct all the mistakes Jacques had made. Jacques didn't like Thursdays.

This lunch time, though, when he got back from the Cafe he found a vase of flowers on his desk, and Madame Pinot was humming to herself as she want through the book of ticket sales. Most odd.

Jacques sat down to think; last week she had given him a jar of home made jam. Now it was flowers. Surely she couldn't be trying to soften him up? Jacques was a confirmed bachelor. He liked being a bachelor; he liked being able to stagger home from the Cafe at all hours, being able to leave the washing up until tomorrow or the day after, being able to do as little shopping as possible. The thought of Madame Pinot, who had been a widow now for some five years, having an eye on him didn't bear thinking about.

He shook himself; it wasn't possible, he must be imagining things. Why him, for heaven's sake? There were plenty of other poor sods out there for her to go after. He went outside for a walk around the station and to clear his head. It was a beautiful day, and all should have been well with the world. When it was five o'clock and the train to Verton had left, it would again be a beautiful day as far as Jacques was concerned.

When he went back inside to finish the letter he had begun before lunch, Mme Pinot was in his office. She had put right the six mistakes in the arithmetic in the ticket sales book, and was now going to go through the goods accounts which included the boxes of shellfish that went out by passenger train.

"Ah, Monsieur Jacques, there you are. What a lovely day, is it not? Such a shame to be in here like this, but duty calls!". With that, she skipped - positively skipped - out of the office.

Jacques collapsed in his chair, a worried man.

The following week it was more flowers and a jar of chutney. The week after that, a bottle of home made wine....to be fair, he had no objection to people giving him wine............and then more damn flowers. It was getting ridiculous.

Summer was blooming by this time, and St Jean looked at its best. The tourist trade was healthy and the railway was kept busy running longer trains than usual with every coach that could turn a wheel being pressed into service. The farmers were happy, the hoteliers were happy, even the fishermen were happy. Only Jacques was miserable; it was Thursday again.

When Mme. Pinot got down from the Verton train at two o'clock Jacques was just walking back from lunch, and he didn't realise who it was until she called a greeting and pushed open the door of the station. He stopped in his tracks. Madame Pinot, that efficient, bossy, terrifying widow woman was wearing a short brightly coloured flowered dress with red sandals and looking positively feminine! Jacques was as French as the next man, he could recognise femininity at a hundred paces, but even so this was the most appalling sight. Why would she suddenly have decided to dress like that, if not to impress him? What on earth was he going to do?

That afternoon, she asked him to have lunch on Sunday. He was desolated, but he had to visit his sister in Amiens. Dinner in the evening? Sadly, he would not be back in time, otherwise of course he would have loved to.

Never mind, she would see him next week on Thursday.

The following week, Jacques took the cowards way out; he felt that it was necessary for him to visit his colleague at Le Crotoy to discuss serious matters of business, so he hopped onto the 11.45 train which left just before the train from Verton carrying Mme. Pinot arrived at St. Jean. Sadly due to the important business requiring his undivided attention it would be impossible for him to return to St Jean before 5.30, by which time Mme. Pinot would have left. All the books had been left ready for her, he was sure she would manage without him.

The problem was that he couldn't keep doing it, at some point he was going to have to be there in his office on a Thursday afternoon. He was losing sleep thinking about it; what on earth could he do?

The solution came to him one morning walking to work from his cottage at the top of Rue les Moulins. His route took him past the Cafe where the crane had got stuck, and sitting outside drinking a coffee was young Marianne.

"Bonjour, Mademoiselle Marianne, a beautiful morning is it not?" Jacques called cheerfully - he was cheerful, it wasn't a Thursday - as he strolled past.

Seeing Marianne made him think; Louis was right, you wouldn't think she was only sixteen. Nature had been bountiful! As he walked on, a plan began to form in his mind. That evening, instead of going for a glass of wine in the Cafe Pierre as usual, he went to the Cafe de Picardie where Marianne lived and helped serve. He went back the following night, and the night after that he had a quiet word with Marianne over a bottle of the best red.

Thursday afternoon came around as Thursday afternoons do, and again Mme Pinot was dressed to impress. Not only that, this time there were flowers and a bottle of wine! Jacques put the wine out of harms way.

Mme. Pinot usually worked in the booking hall behind the counter, sitting on a high stool, and at half past two Jacques wandered in to make sure all the posters were up to date and not in need of replacing.

Mme. Pinot looked up; Jacques looked remarkably relaxed this afternoon, not tense like he usually seemed. Poor man, she thought, he must work too hard, it was not healthy for him. Good heavens, he was actually whistling as he replaced a torn timetable on the wall.

As he was doing so, the door from the street was flung open, and a young girl ran into the station, a young girl in a very short, indeed shockingly short skirt and a very low cut blouse.

"Papa!" she shrieked, and flung her arms around Jacques! Madame Pinot dropped her pen; she seemed to be frozen.

"My six brothers and sisters all bring you their warmest greetings, and Mama says she hopes you are keeping well and not drinking too much wine. Georges will be out of prison soon, little Maria is pregnant and Suzette has run away with a sailor - again" Marianne gushed breathlessly. "When will you come to see us all, Papa, we miss you?"

The young girl then planted a big kiss on Jacques' cheek, walked out through the platform doors and got onto the waiting Le Crotoy train. Madame Pinot could not see her climb down from the train on the other side, walk along the quayside and back into town to the cafe, well pleased with her performance and the easiest twenty francs she had ever earned.

With commendable restraint, Jacques finished putting up the new timetable and then walked slowly back to his office. He did not show any emotion until the door was closed, but then he collapsed in his chair as though he had been punctured. Phew! The only question now was, had it worked?

A week passed slowly, taken up with everyday concerns, and on Thursday promptly at two o'clock the train from Verton pulled into the station. Jacques was already in his office, looking out of the window. Where was Madame Pinot? More to the point, what would she be wearing?

Ah, there she was, and all seemed to be well.........she had on her dark suit, severe and plain, and she was carrying neither flowers or wine. Jacques made sure he was in the booking hall to greet her when she came through the door, and she was distant to the point of being brusque. Jacques went back into the office and danced a jig around his desk; it looked as though he was safe! What a beautiful day it was; suddenly, every bird in Picardie seemed to be singing! He went outside, really one could not be confined in an office on an afternoon as wonderful as this.

That evening he was again in the Cafe de Picardie; it seemed only fair to let Marianne know how successful she had been. She should be on the stage, that one, such a talent was wasted serving in the Cafe!

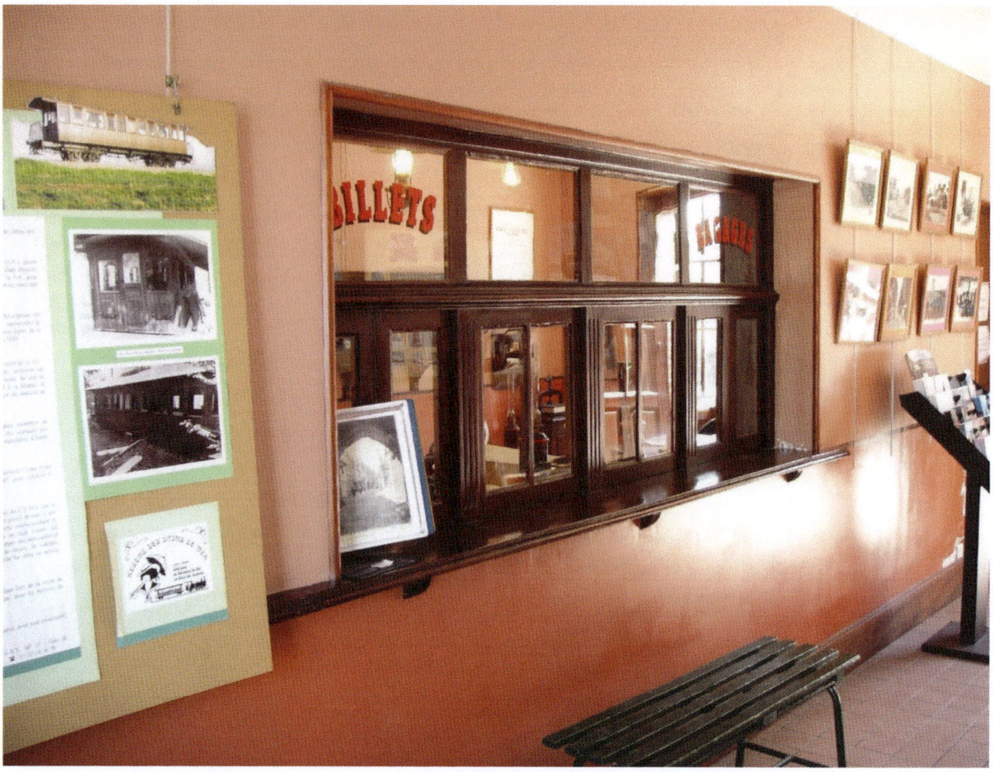
BILLETS

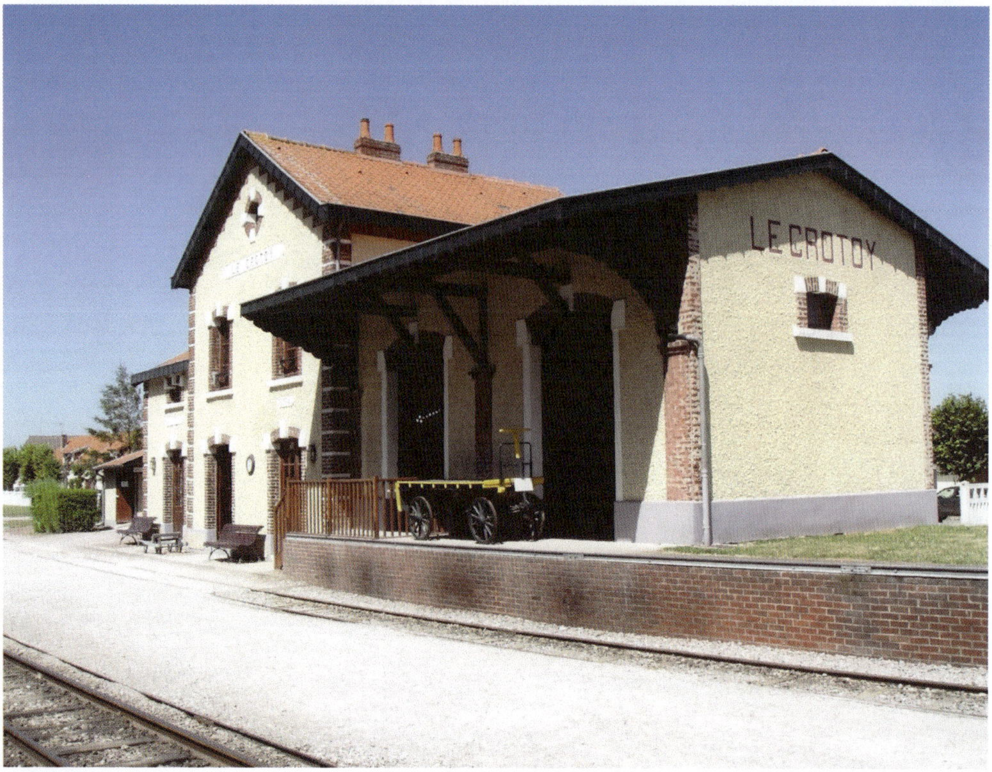
LE CROTOY

Chapter 8

THE FILM

The phone call from M. Artois came early on Friday morning; a company from Paris were making a feature film and wanted to include some scenes on a narrow gauge railway….our narrow gauge railway as it happens. I suggested your station, so they'll be arriving in the morning and are likely to be there all day, so make sure you cooperate with them fully.

Thanks for the warning, thought Jacques. I've got a station to run, I don't want to be falling over these film people all day long. More details filtered through over the course of the day; a special train was being provided for them which would be based at St Jean; as there was no goods traffic on a Saturday it shouldn't present any difficulty. Just leave them to get on with things, they shouldn't get in your way.

When Jacques arrived at the station to open up the following morning two large trucks and a bus were standing in the yard, and a number of people were milling about pointing things out to each other and making suggestions. Jacques had put on his best uniform and was looking quite smart so it was clear who he was as soon as he walked up to the station building; one of the people on the quayside separated from the group he was with and walked up to Jacques, hand outstretched.

"Monsieur, I am pleased to meet you. Monsieur Artois told us all about you. You mustn't worry about us, I know you have a railway to run so treat it as a normal day and we'll try not to get in your way. I am Fred Orain, the producer of this film. Our train will be arriving soon, once that is here was can begin setting up the shots we'll need and hopefully everything will be finished in one day. The weather looks as though it being kind to us so all should be well!"

With that, he walked off.

Jacques wondered around the station in something of a daze until the special train arrived, three coaches pulled by an unusually clean number 4. The special was parked on the siding along the quayside as the other two tracks would be needed for the service trains during the day. Once the special was safely stowed the film crew began to swarm all over it, putting up lights, running cables out to the trucks and generally looking efficient and business like. No one had told Jacques exactly what the film was about or who was in it, and frankly he wasn't particularly bothered…he hadn't been to the cinema for years. He got on with the business of running the station and by mid morning he had almost forgotten about the filming. Mme Artur had arrived to work in the booking office, looking unusually decorative this morning, and for some reason she had her daughter Marie with her. Then Mme Jules arrived; she didn't start work until 2 o'clock, what was she doing here now? Jacques went out to see what was going on.

The two women and Marie were deep in conversation. Jacques was about to enquire what was happening when the waiting room door opened and a man came in, smoking a pipe. Mme Jules screamed!

"Er, excuse me, but I wondered if there might be a toilet in here that I could use? The one on the station is a bit basic!"

"Oh yes, that's perfectly all right, you can use the staff toilet; it's in here" Mme Artur was positively blushing.

"What is going on?" demanded Jacques. "Who's that bloke that thinks he's too good to use the station facilities?"

"Don't you know who he is?" Mme Jules gasped…."That's Jacques Tati, he's the star of the film they are making here today, M. Hulot's Journey".

"Never heard of him", Jacques said and made for the sanctuary of his office.

Things stayed calm until lunch time when Jacques was about to sneak away to the Café. The last morning passenger train had been and gone so there was a period now with nothing pressing to be done. As he put on his jacket there was a knock at the door, and the producer put his head round.

"Ah, there you are. We've done all the shots we need inside the train, so now we'd like to do some action shots of the train moving. What we want to do is run the train out of the station so we can film it coming back in again – I assume that will be all right? I understand that there are no trains due until after two o'clock?"

Well, what could he do? Jacques agreed and came outside to see that everything was being done correctly. This was his station and if it was going to be in a film he was going to see to it that nothing unrailwaylike was happening.

The loco crew tooted the whistle, and the little engine backed the coaches out of the station, past the loco shed and water tank until they were out of sight. The director had a radio and presumably someone on the train had too so that they could communicate with one another. The cameras were readied, the director gave the word and the locomotive burst into life, trundling round the curve past the shed in a cloud of steam. Then the sun went behind a cloud.

The second attempt was better, except that this time there was so much steam the locomotive was invisible inside its own personal cloud…..words were had and the crew were told to close the cylinder drain cocks on the next run. The train was backed up for another attempt. The third try went really well, the train ran into the station looking resplendent and came to a halt in exactly the right place. Then there was a pause….M. Hulot was supposed to climb down from the train and walk into the station. He was nowhere to be seen. At that moment he came out of the station….unknown to everyone he had popped into use the facilities again. The director began to look harassed.

Jacques stood watching as the little train was backed out of the station for the fourth time. As he watched he was aware of someone standing beside him, also watching. A young woman, no one Jacques had seen before.

"They are trying again" commented Jacques. "This time let's hope they get it right!"

The woman smiled but didn't speak; the train began to move and this time everything went like clockwork until the second that M. Hulot stepped off the carriage step at which moment the safety valves on the locomotive lifted, drowning out all sound and ruining the shot. The director looked as though he wished he'd used a diesel.

"My God!" said Jacques, "If it took me this many times to run a train into the station we'd have no passengers left". The young woman smiled again, and then as the train backed out for the fifth attempt she walked across to the director and spoke to him.

This time the sun stayed out, the locomotive behaved and M. Hulot walked unimpeded into the station building where Mme. Jules had made him a cup of coffee.

Next the director wanted to put the locomotive on the other end of the train so that he could film it departing the station; that would take time, as all the cables lying across the tracks would have to be moved. Jacques was beginning to worry; between two o'clock and half past two passenger trains were due to arrive and depart and they were more important than any damn film. The director was giving orders; number 4 was uncoupled and ran to the end of the station so the points could be changed. As it did so the whistle of the first passenger train was heard and all filming had to be stopped while the normal life of the station continued.

The trains were busy and a lot of people who had got off stayed on the station to see what was going on, so that after the second train had left the area in front of the station building was still crowded. The director was getting frazzled again.

He gave a signal that all was ready, the Number 4 have a toot on her whistle and then trundled slowly along the centre track towards the water tower. As it did so there was a touch on Jacques' arm; it was Marianne from the Café Picardie asking after a parcel her father was expecting. As the loco ran past Marianne gave a gasp; she was looking at the young women Jacques had been talking to earlier on.

"That's Nathalie Pascaud!" Marianne shrieked.

"Who?" asked Jacques, to whom the name of the famous French film actress meant nothing.

"Do you meant you've never heard of her?" demanded Marianne. "Do you lock yourself in a box when you go home?!"

While they were talking the train had been coupled together ready to leave, and the director was looking in their direction. He wasn't looking at Jacques, he was looking at Marianne. He walked across, with Nathalie Pascaud alongside him.

"Enchante Mademoiselle", he said, ignoring Jacques. "I wonder….we need some people for this scene, and I wondered if you would care to help us out? I need a young woman to stand on the balcony of the first coach, waving as the train leaves the station….could you do that for me? Nathalie will take you to make-up and show you what to do"

Walking on air, Marianne was lead across to the large bus in the station yard. In the meantime the cameras were all arranged in new positions in order to film the train leaving the station. The director came back across to Jacques….would he be good enough to stand by the train waving his flag as it left the station? Jacques didn't like to tell him that it was not the job of the Chef de Gare to wave a flag at departing trains, he simply agreed to stand where he was told. Once all was ready and Marianne was in position on the front coach ready to wave to M. Hulot as the train left, the director gave the signal to proceed.

This time it only took four attempts to get a take that could be used.

By five o'clock the film crew were winding down, happy with the shots they had got and ready to remove all their equipment. M. Artois had arrived on the afternoon train from Verton to see how it was all going and he seemed pleased that there had been no mishaps to reflect badly on the railway. The two stars had gone, but the director and his assistants had decided to stay in the town overnight; apparently they needed to film some scenes in a café, and someone had told them how perfect the Cafe Picardie would be so tomorrow they would be having a look and discussing the possibilities with the owner…and his daughter.

Monsieur Hulot's Journey was released the following Spring, and of course it was shown at the small cinema in St Jean sur Mer. For once Jacques had been persuaded to go and to his amazement there he was, larger than life, flagging off the departing passenger train as Marianne waved from the front of the leading coach. The scenes that had taken all day to film at the station lasted less than thirty seconds on the film, but it was still nice to see it. As for the Café Picardie, although the interior shots were done back in the studio the Café was unmistakable and it did business no harm at all.

Chapter 9

CHICKENS

The train from Le Crotoy arrived promptly by Cote de Picardie standards; it was only five minutes late. The guard jumped down from his Fourgon, and when the passengers were safely out of the way he came into the station building looking for Jacques.

"I've got a crate of chickens in the van", he said. "Some farmer is meant to be collecting them. What do you want me to do with them in the meantime?".

"How big is the crate?" asked Jacques. "We can't bring it in here if it's a big one, it will have to go in the goods shed. It will be cooler in there too."

"It's not the size that's the problem," replied the guard, "It's the condition. The damn thing is nearly falling apart and I'll need some help carrying it. Is there anyone around that can give me a hand?".

The two men walked outside, but the station was deserted apart from the locomotive crew preparing to run round their train with the engine. There was no one else in the station building, and the goods shed was empty as the two porters were out delivering parcels in the town.

"Looks like you and me, then" grunted Jacques. They walked towards the Fourgon and the Guard slid open the side door. Inside on the floor was a large wooden crate which had certainly seen better days. Inside there seemed to be around half a dozen chickens, all of them making enough noise to wake the dead. The label on the crate said a name Jacques didn't know and an address a couple of kilometres outside the town. Presumably the farmer, whoever he was, would drive in to collect his chickens before long.

"The goods shed it is, then. It will be out of the sun for them in there."

The two of them slid the heavy crate to the edge of the Fourgon; the next thing was to get it to ground level. It was about a metre square, roughly nailed together several decades ago by the look of it. The hinged lid was simply tied in place with baling string.

"Farmers! Never spend a Franc if they can help it." The Guard commented as they pulled the crate so that half of it was outside the door. The chickens had stopped making a noise and were looking interested, pecking the fingers of Jacques and the Guard in a playful way. With another heave, the crate scraped forwards another fifty centimetres, and as the two men held tightly onto the sides the bottom fell out, along with six chickens.

Jacques and the Guard stood there holding the remains of the crate as the chickens celebrated their new found freedom by disappearing in all directions in search of something tasty to eat.

"Merde! Put this thing down, quickly, after them!" shouted Jacques.

"What do we do with then once we've caught them?" the guard responded. "No good putting them back in here."

"God! Why me?" asked Jacques despairingly. It was almost lunch time, and here he was on a wild chicken hunt when he should have been thinking about the Cafe.

In the goods shed was a large wooden box, nice and solid with a proper hinged lid and holes in the sides as handles. They took out the car parts that it contained, and in their place put the straw from the crate. They put the box ready next to the Fourgon with the lid propped open.......right, now for the chickens.

Jacques set off towards the engine shed, the Guard along the quayside in the opposite direction; he could see one chicken already, pecking at something on the ground outside the Harbour Master's office.

There was no similar target near the engine shed, only the seagulls overhead and the ducks in the harbour were remotely bird like. Jacques climbed the ladder up the side of the water tower to get a better view over the whole station. Hah! There was one, behind the coaling stage. He went after it quickly before it could vanish, and came back a couple of minutes later triumphantly holding it under one arm. True, his uniform was now black & blue rather than blue all over and he had a large smudge on one cheek, but he did have a chicken. The guard was approaching too, similarly encumbered by his chicken, and into the box the two went.

A shout attracted their attention; the locomotive driver, a big grin on his face, was approaching them holding a struggling chicken upside down by its legs.

"Have you lost this?" he chuckled, "I was going to have it for my dinner, but if you want it back....."

Three found, three to go.

The other three, of course, were less easily captured. They decided to hunt together this time, and the loco crew joined in, not wanting to miss the fun. A few passengers had begun to arrive but they had nearly ten minutes before they were due to leave. Jacques wasn't sure if anyone was selling tickets in the station, but he didn't have the time to care. Madame Jules was meant to be in the booking office by now, she worked there in the afternoons, but he wasn't going to go and look. What if that farmer arrived before they had rounded up all the chickens?

"There's one!" A triumphant cry from the fireman, who was off after it before they could say anything. The chicken saw him coming, and calmly took to the air, flying across the harbour and landing on a mud bank in the water surrounded by ducks & geese.

"You idiot, you frightened it!" Jacques shouted, "How the hell do we get it back from there?".

"We don't", answered the Guard, "We've a train to take out and it's due to depart in five minutes. I'm sorry, the chicken's are all yours. Tell me tomorrow how you got on .....if you have caught them by then, of course!"

The Guard and the loco crew walked chuckling back to the train leaving Jacques standing on the quayside looking at the chicken on the mud bank, which was looking back at Jacques. It looked a very smug chicken, a very self satisfied chicken indeed.

An hour later, Jacques had caught the two more chickens from the station side of the river. He had looked for a fisherman with a dinghy that could row him across to the mud bank, but the fishermen were all at sea. The only people around seemed to be tourists who had the leisure time to stop and enjoy the sight of a station master scurrying after chickens on a hot afternoon. They made helpful comments, they asked him if he knew there was a chicken on the mud bank over there......what they didn't do was offer to help, watching was much more fun.

The train from Verton pulled into the station as Jacques was still standing on the quayside, train full of curious passengers with Louis and Maurice on the engine. Oddly enough, they were not inclined to help get the errant chicken back either, but they did offer to hold Jacques' coat for him if he wanted to go for a paddle.

Much later that afternoon, the phone rang. Jacques was in his office, but Madame Jules answered the telephone in the booking hall; she only bothered Jacques when a call was important.

Jacques could hear her from his office, but on this occasion he decided not to get involved.

"Bonjour, St Jean sur Mer station. How may I help you?" asked Mme Jules. "Yes, Monsieur, you collected a box of chickens this afternoon, they were delivered earlier on from Le Crotoy, yes, I understand. What is the problem?"

"There was a duck in the box! Five chickens and a duck! Monsieur, what are you saying; why would anyone send you a duck? That is a ridiculous idea, surely who ever sent them must know the difference!".

"Monsieur, I assure you, if they arrived by train they would simply have been unloaded and stored until collected, we do not open boxes that are being delivered to our customers. You need to take this up with the person that sent them to you, not us. We simply transport whatever we are given. I take it the label on the box was correct? Well, then, there is nothing more to be said".

Thank God I remembered the label at the last moment, thought Jacques, it would have been difficult to explain if they had arrived saying 'car parts'.

"Monsieur, I assure you that this is not a matter for the railway", Madame Jules was saying firmly, "If you have been sent the wrong items it is a matter for the sender and it is him that you must approach to complain. Really, the very idea that a chicken could transform itself into a duck on one of our trains is quite ridiculous, I am surprised at you for suggesting it. You are looking for compensation, I imagine; well, Monsieur, you are looking in the wrong place!".

And with that, she put down the phone.

"What a woman!" thought Jacques; I would have admitted everything and offered to buy him a whole yard full of chickens within thirty seconds.

It was nearly time to close up the station; the last train would be arriving any minute and Madame Jules had her coat on ready to walk home. She said goodbye and went out of the door, but almost at once she came back in again.

"Monsieur Jacques, come and look at this", she said, "Are my eyes deceiving me, or is there a chicken sitting with the ducks on the mud bank across the harbour?" She was looking very hard at Jacques, as only a woman can.

They went outside, and Jacques made a great show of peering at the mud bank, but no, he couldn't see anything at all odd there, nothing at all. A trick of the light, Madame, or perhaps a small goose?

Chapter 10

A VISIT FROM 'LES ANGLAIS'

One Saturday in June that year would long be remembered by the residents of St Jean sur Mer; it was the day the English came to town.

M. Artois had received a letter a couple of months earlier asking if it would be possible for a visit to the Cote de Picardie to be arranged by the Locomotive Club of Great Britain. They would like to hire a train and travel over the whole line if possible, with steam traction of course. They would arrive at Verton by train after spending the night in Boulogne and spend the day on the line before catching the last train north on the main line in the evening. They anticipated bringing around sixty members on the trip, the letter said.

M. Artois worked out how much money these crazy English were likely to spend, rubbed his hands together and rang Jacques to tell him what to expect. The party would be having lunch at St Jean, he had better warn the Cafe's.

The problem presented by the trip was that it was now the height of the tourist season and this special train would have to be fitted around the service trains. Furthermore, most of the serviceable coaches were already in use as the Autorail wasn't big enough to cope with the extra Summer passengers so every vehicle that could turn a wheel would have to be pressed into service. At least on a Saturday there were no goods trains to get in the way, and that freed a locomotive for the special without having to drag one out of the works and prepare it.

St Jean was already buzzing; the weather had been superb and the town was making the most of it. Jacques had arranged to borrow Marianne from the Cafe Picardie for the day as she had been studying English at school and would be able to translate for him. She should also be a good advertisement for the undoubted supremacy of French women, thought Jacques!

On the morning of the visit the staff at St Jean had plenty of time to prepare as the special train was not due to leave Verton until 10.30, and it would only be reversing at St Jean before heading off to Le Crotoy. Only when it returned at 12.30 would things get busy, as the train was not due to leave again until 2.30; in the meantime, it would be clogging up one of the loops at the station while the sixty Englishmen would be happily drinking St Jean dry if what he had heard about them was true. He had to get them all back on the train in time for it to leave as the schedule was tight, they had to get to Berck and back to Verton in time for their main line connection. Worst of all, because of when they were arriving it looked as if Jacques was not going to get any lunch!

He got the phone call from Verton at 10.35 to say that the Special had just left; a loco, a Fourgon and three coaches. The coaches had been taken from the scrap sidings behind the works but they were all there was and the English apparently thought they were wonderful. They had used three on the assumption that at least one of them was bound to fall to pieces before the day was out.

When the train whistled for the footpath crossing by the trestle, Jacques, Marianne and a large crowd of curious onlookers were standing in front of the station building. The loco whistled again and swung over the points and into the station, coming to halt on the centre road. As soon as it did so, people were jumping off the coaches and out of the Fourgon, scrambling to photograph the loco as it uncoupled and ran round. They all ignored Jacques, what's more they all ignored Marianne - he was flabbergasted! It was only the old number 4, a Corpet Louvet like the others, what was so exciting about that? With a cheery whistle the loco ran to the end of the headshunt without running down any of the visitors, then eased its way back over the point and along the loop line. A swarm of men kept pace with it, laden with cameras, sweating in their sports jackets....some were even wearing ties. Truly a remarkable race, the English, thought Jacques.

At that moment, he sensed a presence next to him, and turning he saw a tall thin man with two cameras round his neck and a light meter in his hand. The man said something incomprehensible to him, so Jacques stepped to one side and pushed Marianne forward. She smiled sweetly and the man dropped his light meter. Marianne bent over to pick it up for him, and he dropped a notebook and two pencils..........for some reason he had gone bright red.

"Good morning, Monsieur, welcome to St Jean sur Mer" said Marianne.

"I say, gosh, absolutely!" answered the man. "I'm Thompson, John Thompson. I organised this little jaunt".

"This is Monsieiur Jacques Rodin, the Chef de Gare here at St Jean". Marianne gestured towards Jacques, and the tall Englishman grabbed him by the hand and shook it warmly.

"Delighted, monsieur, delighted!" he cried.

57

By the time they had established that Mr Thompson was in fact very organised and fully aware of the need to keep to their timetable, the loco had been coupled to the end of the train and was whistling furiously to tell the visitors to get back on board, it was time to go.

"We will see you again at lunch time", Marianne called loudly as the train gathered pace out of the station,. For the first time, the English seemed to realise that there was more to look at here than the train, and at least thirty of them were hanging off the last coach trying to get a last look at Marianne as it passed the loco shed and ran out of the station, heading for Le Crotoy.

Peace descended again, and Jacques and Marianne went into the station for a cup of coffee. Heaven knew what was going to happen when they arrived back from Le Crotoy, thought Jacques. Oddly enough, Marianne seemed to be quite looking forward to it.

The morning passed quietly, until a distant whistle alerted them to the return of the special train. In fact there seemed to be rather a lot of whistling, far more than was strictly necessary for one little footpath and as the train ran into the station he could see why, there were at least four Englishmen hanging out of the cab of the loco, cheering and blowing the whistle madly.

"My God" thought Jacques, "What have we done to deserve this?"

As before, he was ignored as the mass of enthusiasts dispersed to photograph the train, the station, the quayside, each other.......they clambered onto the coal stage, up the water tower, into wagons, all trying to get that one photograph that would be better than everyone else's. As it became clear that the loco was not going to move again for at least an hour, the thought of lunch began to impress itself on the crowd, and Mr Thompson again approached Jacques & Marianne.

No one cafe in the town could take so many visitors at once, but if they would like to walk up the main street there were plenty of places ready to welcome them. Naturally Marianne made sure that the Cafe Picardie was mentioned more than once.

Oddly enough, when he looked around when the majority of the English had gone Marianne was nowhere to be seen; very strange. Shaking his head, Jacques walked back into the sanctuary of his office where there was a bottle of Cognac in the safe.

It was the singing that he noticed first; very loud, very raucous and coming nearer as he listened. He went out of the station; it was coming from the Rue des Moulins and leading it was a girls voice. As Jacques looked, round the corner of the station approach came a group of about twenty of the younger Englishmen lead by Marianne who was looking as though she might have just enjoyed a very good lunch indeed. The group finished their song, which being in English meant nothing to Jacques, and headed for the quayside where they arranged themselves in a ragged group with Marianne in the middle. She called to Jacques to come and take their photograph.

Jacques walked across, feeling conspicuous in his best uniform, and took the first of the proffered cameras. The other cameras were placed to one side to be used in turn; the group, in three lines, grinned at him. It was then that Jacques had a very wicked thought.

There are times when speech is not necessary; this was one such occasion. Jacques made a great show of looking though the viewfinder & composing the photograph, but the group was just not far enough back.........he indicated with his hand that one more pace backwards would make it perfect. They all stepped back one pace, and the back row of five Englishmen disappeared into the harbour with a shout and a great splash!

Pandemonium broke out. Marianne was laughing uncontrollably, the loco crew watching from their footplate were in the same state, and Jacques was hoping he hadn't drowned anyone. Lifebelts were flung into the harbour, ropes were thrown and five very wet and embarrassed visitors scrambled up the iron ladders that were placed at intervals along the harbour wall to stand dripping on the quayside.

Happily it was a very warm day and before long they were drying out in the sun, and Marianne was making sure that none of them were hurt; indeed she was showing the greatest possible concern. No harm at been done, and it had given the dry members of the party something to remember for a long time even if the damp ones might wish to forget it rather more quickly.

A whistle from the engine told them that it was time to go; the offer of a footplate ride to the involuntary swimmers had cheered them up, as had a goodbye kiss to each of them from Marianne............was it Jacque's imagination or had one of them managed to get two kisses? Not that Marianne seemed to mind, he thought.

Chapter 11

FIRE AND WATER

That Wednesday morning had begun uneventfully enough, just another day on the Cote de Picardie. Business was brisk, the weather was benevolent and it wasn't a Thursday so Jacques could relax safe in the knowledge that he wouldn't be seeing Mme Pinot today. All was well with the world. With his feet on his desk, Jacques lay back in his chair and sipped his coffee as he listened to the sounds of the harbour drifting through the open window of his office; it was a hard life at times!

This peaceful scene was interrupted when his office door was flung open and Louis came in, red faced and panting.

"There's no water coming out of the tank" he gasped, having run to the station from the water tower, all of 100 metres. "Our loco is almost out of water, we need to fill her up".

The two men rushed outside to the water tower where Maurice was frantically pulling the chain that should have sent a jet of water cascading into the side tanks of the locomotive. Today though, there was nothing. Jacques looked up at the tank – on the side was an indicator that showed the level of water in the tank and it was showing that there wasn't any; the tank was empty. It had been working perfectly well last night; why hadn't the tank filled up as it should do automatically when the level dropped? It was fed from a deep borehole with a pump to raise the water up to the cylindrical tank on top of the stone tower. The water tank was one of those things that one never really gave a thought to, it was always there and it always worked, it was as simple as that.

Until today.

Louis was starting to panic; there wasn't enough water in the locomotive's tanks to run back to Verton to fill up and they needed water urgently. If the tanks ran dry the fire would have to be dumped or the boiler would be damaged, and that would mean that the engine would be out of action for the rest of the day. Jacques looked at the harbour….plenty of water there. Louis soon put him right; you can't put salt water into a steam locomotive without causing serious damage, they needed fresh water, and quickly.

There were three fire buckets hanging on the wall of the station building; these were brought into use, one filled from the kitchen sink in the station, one from the tap in the loco shed and the third from the sink in the ladies toilet which happily was not occupied when Jacques rushed in. Between them they kept a chain going as people arriving at the station came forward to help and more buckets were found; gradually the level in the side tanks began to rise. Louis began to look a bit less white faced; his locomotive was going to be all right. Half an hour later…and half an hour late….he was able to back onto his train and steam out of the station for Le Crotoy, where there was a big water tank that hopefully would be working properly.

Once the train had gone Jacques rang Verton to inform them of what had happened and why the train was so late and they promised to send out a man to look at the pump in the water tower to check that it was working correctly. In the meantime all locomotives would be told to fill up their tanks at Verton or Le Crotoy so they should have enough water for the whole trip.

Jacques was just beginning to think about lunch when he heard a shouting from outside; looking through the office window he could see a figure in blue overalls running up the track towards the station, shouting as he came. Jacques went outside, pausing to put on his jacket and cap, to meet the energetic person, whoever he was. As he got closer Jacques recognised the goods guard from Verton. Whatever could be wrong?

The guard was slowing down now – it was a hot day – and as he staggered past the water tower he began gesticulating to Jacques, who went to meet him.

"Water!" he shouted. "We need water – we've a wagon on fire!"

He panted out his story – he was the guard of the morning goods from Verton, and behind the loco they had three wagons of straw, covered in tarpaulins. A spark for the engine had got under one of the tarpaulins and set fire to the straw which was now well ablaze…they needed to bring the train into the station under the water tank so the water from the tank could be used to put out the flames. They had tried to put the fire out themselves but the flames was too fierce and the wooden wagon body was burning too; they had uncoupled the rest of the train, and the driver was going to bring the loco and the three wagons into the station. Claude paused; they could hear the sound of a locomotive and smoke was rising in the distance.

Well, they had picked the wrong day. Jacques explained to the guard the situation with the water tank, that the only supply they had was a hosepipe from the Gentlemen's toilet and that wasn't enough to put out a match, let along three blazing wagons of straw. The guard looked at him ashen faced; as they stood there the locomotive trundled into view with its blazing train close behind…..the loco was whistling frantically and the crew were hanging on the steps on either side. With no back to the cab things were getting too hot for comfort. Fortunately the wagon next to the engine was as yet not fully ablaze but the other were going really well by now, with smoke rising in a thick cloud. The train juddered to a halt under the tank.

"Turn on the water!" shouted the driver.

"Turn on the water!" shouted the driver.

"Take the damn things out of my bloody station" shouted Jacques. "You'll burn down the whole place!"

The guard rushed up to tell the driver what had happened, that there was no water.

"Push them back up the line, quickly" Jacques yelled.

That was the obvious thing to do, but there was a problem….pulling the train the loco crew had been in front of the flames, but pushing them from the back, that was a different matter, they would have no protection at all. The train was there, and it was staying there. The driver uncoupled his locomotive and drew it forwards out of harm's way while Jacques ran to phone the town fire brigade. When he got back things were settling down; two of the wagons had pretty much burnt out and the third was being kept under control with more buckets of water and the hose pipe, now connected to the engine shed tap. Using water straight from the harbour wasn't a problem now, so the buckets were being filled with sea water. There was a lot of smoke from the damp straw, but the flames were dying down so that when the fire brigade arrived and drove their fire engine along the quayside to the wagons most of the excitement was already over.

Once all three wagons had been given a good soaking and the fire was out, the next problem confronted them; the wagons were standing in front of the water tower on the main line & blocking the station and a passenger train was due from le Crotoy in ten minutes. The goods train locomotive was OK so it was backed onto the smouldering wagons and very gingerly they were pushed along the line and then pulled to the far end of the quayside siding where one of them finally expired in a heap of charred timber and blackened metal. That was going to be a job for the breakdown crew form Verton; Jacques went into the station building to report to M. Artois what had happened. The next problem was the rest of the freight train which was still standing on the main line to Verton without a locomotive. The goods loco was stranded behind the three burnt out wagons so that couldn't be used, and the passenger train was due to leave for Verton as soon as it arrived…..in fact Jacques could hear it now. Verton acted quickly; they sent out the Locotracteur to collect the stranded wagons and take them back to Verton so the passenger train was only delayed for twenty minutes, a not uncommon occurrence of the Cote de Picardie anyway.

It was early afternoon by now, Jacques hadn't had any lunch and still the station had no water supply. He went back out to the water tank and opened the door in the base of the stone tower which supported the cylindrical iron tank. The pump looked OK, but Jacques was no expert. Verton were sending out a fitter; he'd have to wait until he arrived.

Walking back to the station Jacques noticed that the sun had gone in; a huge black cloud was looming over St Jean sur Mer. As he opened the door into the station came the first crack of thunder and the heaven's opened. For the next half an hour curtains of rain were blown across the harbour and it bounced off the granite sets of the station; the holidaymakers rushed for the cafes, the locals headed home and Jacques sat gloomily looking out at the scene; isn't it typical, he thought, when you want water there's none to be had but when you don't, you get this lot.

When the storm had passed Jacques ventured out again; normal business was resumed and later in the afternoon a man came to see what had happened to the water tank. Jacques left him to get on with it; when he came back to the station an hour later he explained that the pump had packed up but he'd got it going again and the tank was filling up nicely so they'd soon be able to use it again. What they really needed was a new pump, but the chances of Verton paying for that were about the same as the odds on Jacques getting a pay rise. At least normal service had been resumed; he didn't like disruptions, they were bad for the digestion.

Chapter 12

THE HARBOUR MASTER MISSES LUNCH

The brick built building that contained the office of the Harbour Master at St Jean sur Mer had stood at the end of the quayside for over two hundred years. The Harbour Master was an important man; his office with its imposing bow windows commanded a clear view across the estuary of the Authie and along the whole of the quayside. At one time the harbour would have been busy with coastal sailing ships but now only fishing boats and the occasional yacht tied up alongside the stone wall. Nevertheless a harbour master was still required, the rules still had to be followed and the tolls collected.

When the railway was being built in the 1890's there was a lot of discussion about the siting of the station, but in the end the quayside had been the obvious place; otherwise a separate line to the quay would have to be built and why go to that expense? So it was that the station stood on the quayside, and the sidings ran parallel with the harbour wall for the convenience of loading & unloading the ships.

It was unfortunate that almost as soon as the line opened most of the shipping stopped using St Jean due to silting in the estuary and the lure of busier harbours, but the sidings were still used for general traffic. One of them ran right along the harbour wall and terminated outside the door of the harbour master's office, with only a stout wooden block marking the end of the siding. At first, those using the office for business had looked with some concern at this wooden block which did not seem all that substantial, but as the years passed familiarity had bred contempt and now no one gave it a second glance.

This was rather unfortunate, as sixty years after it had been placed there the part of the wooden block that was buried in the ground was not as solid as it once had been. Not to put too fine a point on it, the block was totally rotten.

On a bright, breezy Monday morning in early July, the station was busy dealing with the newly arrived passenger train from Le Crotoy and the morning goods, the wagons of which had to be shunted into position for loading and unloading, some by the goods shed, two in the loading dock & the remainder on the quay siding. The little Corpet Louvet tank engine huffed and puffed its way around the station getting under the feet of all and sundry, finally propelling the two vans onto the quayside to get them out of the way until they were needed for unloading later in the morning. It was a happy scene, with holidaymakers, fishermen and a few townspeople watching the proceedings and passing the time of day. ....it was always pleasant to watch other people working, after all.

Jacques was standing at the door of the station ready to wave off the passenger train which was now ready to depart, and so couldn't see the goods engine and its vans. Frankly he had forgotten that it existed until a great crash and a fine cloud of grey dust rising into the air brought him running around the rear of the coaches onto the quayside. He stopped dead, unable to comprehend what he was seeing; the goods loco was standing on the siding, but the two vans had taken to their heels, run right through the stop block and embedded themselves in the front of the Harbour Master's Office. There was a brief moment of shocked silence, and then everyone seemed to start talking at once, with two exceptions; the crew of the shunting engine weren't saying anything, they were standing by their engine looking as though they were waiting for the end of the world to arrive. Jacques felt much the same; he forced his legs to carry him towards the pile of wreckage, and the loco crew followed him ………as the three of them stood surveying the devastation the upper window of the Harbour Office opened and a white face looked out at them.

Normally, Monsieur Jules the 'Maitre de Port' was an imposing ruddy faced figure; with his full beard neatly trimmed he looked every centimetre the nautical officer even though he had never sailed beyond Dieppe in his life. At this moment, though, he was looking anything but imposing; had his legs been visible they would certainly have been shaking, and who could blame him for that? Behind him, the even paler face of Madame Minot his secretary could be seen peering out at the gathering crowd of onlookers, which was growing larger with every passing minute.

As befitted his position, Jacques took charge. "Are you both all right?" he called up at them. It was not the right moment to ask; M. Jules had just had a very trying couple of minutes, and now all the pent up emotion that he was feeling was released in a stream of very nautical language, most of it calling into doubt the parentage of Jacques and the loco crew. As M. Jules was one of Jacques best friends, it showed how affected he had been by his office collapsing around his ears without warning as he sipped his morning coffee. When he paused for breath, Jacques asked if anyone else had been in the building, particularly on the ground floor which had taken the brunt of the force, but thankfully there hadn't been.

Jacques walked forward for a better look at the office; the buffer of the first van had smashed through the rotten stop block and had proceeded right through the main door. Unfortunately the rest of the van had been rather wider and had reduced itself to matchwood against the brick walls on either side while the second van did much the same behind it. The twisted metal of the two chassis lay across the paving in front of the office, some of it hanging over the harbour wall. What made things worse was the fact that the two vans had been loaded with sacks of cement powder which had tumbled out of the wreckage, many of them splitting & pouring their contents over the granite setts in front of the office building. A thin layer of grey dust was settling over everything in the vicinity.

The doorway was totally blocked with wreckage, and the upper floor of the building looked as though the only thing keeping it up was the end of the first van which was firmly wedged in place. Even more unfortunate was the fact that the Harbour Office only had one doorway, the one in which the wreckage of the two vans was now sitting.

Someone had had the presence of mind to call the town fire brigade, a term which conjures up an image rather more impressive than the reality, but nevertheless ten minutes later they arrived panting at the quayside with their fire engine, bell ringing and red paint gleaming in the sunshine. Off they piled, and Jacques was glad to be able to leave the rescue of M. Jules and Madame Minot to them. From the way they were standing around scratching their heads and prodding the wreckage, it might take some time.

"Come on", Jacques said to the loco crew. "I've got to phone Verton and tell them what has happened. I hope you've got your excuses ready".

It seemed that to save time, they had propelled the two wagons along the quayside siding without coupling them to the engine, a practice that was far from unheard of. On this occasion, though, they had given the two vans a harder shove than they had intended to and the fireman had not been able to run after them in order to put down the brake handle. Off they had careered along the uneven track of the siding, the heavy cement helping them gather momentum as they went.........the stop block would usually have prevented any damage, but they had swept it aside as though it had been made of cardboard and here for all to see was the result. Verton were not going to be pleased!

His phone call completed, Jacques and the loco crew walked back along the quayside; M. Artois was coming down by the next train, which was due in half an hour. Thankfully the rest of the station was undamaged so that normal operations could proceed.

"Put your engine in the shed for the time being", said Jacques.........it would give the two men something to do for a few minutes. They rushed off to do as he had said; the loco would still be needed for the afternoon goods train, what was left of it.

Back at the Harbour Office, M. Jules was leaning precariously out of the upper window. There was a problem; the two bay windows looked directly over the harbour, and there was not sufficient ground between the wall and the quayside for a ladder. Getting a ladder to the front window was even more of a problem due to the pile of wreckage; for the moment, M. Jules and Madame Pinot were trapped in the upper room of the building, and M. Jules was not taking the news at all well. It was nearly lunch time, he could see the Cafe clearly when he leaned out; in fact he was convinced that he could even smell the lunch! Getting to it, however, was going to take rather longer than he desired - today, lunch would be delayed.

His mood was not helped when M. Artois arrived, and he and Jacques headed for the Cafe to discuss what had happened and what to do about it. M. Jules watched them all the way to the door...........damn them, how could they eat at a time like this? Very easily, it seemed.

In the end, the crew of the goods engine were sent off to Verton with their engine to collect a couple of open wagons and the crane truck, with some more men to help with the clear up. Jacques returned to the station to continue with his duties there and M. Artois caught the 3pm train back to his office. Things were settling down; as the wreckage was cleared, the fire brigade propped up the front of the building with timber so that there was no danger of it collapsing. Finally, at a quarter to five they felt able to lean a ladder against the front wall and rescue M Jules and Madame Pinot from their prison. M. Jules immediately went looking for Jacques, but oddly enough Jacques was no where to be found, having conveniently discovered that he had an important appointment in the town that could not wait until the following day.

It took the next couple of days to clear all the debris and hose down the quayside but in the end it was done. A temporary harbour office had been opened in the station building which made things a little strained for a few days, but eventually friendship triumphed over adversity even if it did cost Jacques a small fortune in wine at the Cafe; the tale as told by M. Jules grew more horrendous with every telling until it was on a par with the San Fransisco earthquake!

When the repairs to the Harbour Office were completed later in the Summer the staff at the station rather missed having M. Jules and Madame Pinot around the place, but M. Jules had made it clear that a man of his importance in the town must have his own office in his own building from which to transact his business. Those who had suggested that they didn't actually need a Harbour Master any more - after all, it was 1958 - were put firmly in their place. One thing M. Jules did make certain of..........the siding along the quayside was shortened by twenty metres, and a very solid metal stop block was concreted firmly in place at the end of it.

Chapter 13

THE BULL

A railway such as the Cote de Picardie was a common carrier; in other words whatever traffic was offered it was their job to get it to the destination, whatever it may be. Generally that wasn't a problem; boxes of fruit or fish, some farm machinery, some items for the Hotels or shops in the town; it wasn't an issue, that was what they were there for. The railway goods stock wasn't very specialised, just open wagons for larger items that wouldn't be affected by the weather and vans for perishable produce. There were the Fourgon's for parcels, and a couple of tank wagons for oil and that was about it.

As Chef de Gare Jacques was responsible for the good traffic as well as the passengers, although he generally left the two goods porters Henri & Michel to their own devices. Both had worked at the station for years, they were good steady men who knew their jobs inside out. They unloaded the goods wagons, did the deliveries around the town in between trains, and had outgoing items ready for loading when the goods trains arrived. There was a small goods shed attached to the station building which was a secure place for items to be left overnight if necessary.

One pleasant Thursday morning at the end of June the business of the station was proceeding normally without anything out of the way to concern Jacques, other than the fact that it was Thursday again, the day for checking his books and accounts. The afternoon goods train was due to arrive from Le Crotoy at ten to three and it usually spent an hour or so at St Jean before proceeding to Verton. There had been no special instructions about today's train so when it pulled into the station Jacques didn't give it a thought. When there came a knock on his office door he didn't connect it with the goods train, until Henri looked into the office.

"Er…Jacques…we might need your help for a few minutes. We've got a special delivery and we're not sure what to do about it".

Jacques followed Henri out of the office and round to the goods shed; a covered van had been placed by the shed, in front of which was a raised loading platform. The rest of the goods wagons were spread around the station according to what they carried and whether they were being taken on the Verton, and the goods engine was taking water at the tank. The goods guard was standing by the van with Michel, and both looked worried; the guard had a dispatch card in his hand.

"What's the problem?" asked Jacques, still unconcerned about what looked to be a perfectly normal scene.

Then something kicked the side of the van – hard.

Jacques took a step backwards.

"What the hell have you got in there?" he asked.

"It's a prize bull" replied the guard, "It's being collected by the new owner, a farmer from Rue. They couldn't unload it there because there's no platform. The card says 'to be kept until collected' but it doesn't say where or how. The van has got to be unloaded, they need it taking back to Verton this afternoon".

"Where are we supposed to keep a bull?" demanded Jacques. "We can't put him in the goods shed!"

"There's nowhere else, is there?" asked Henri. "What's more after riding in that van he's going to be hot, he'll need some water. They shouldn't use a van like that for livestock, it's not right".

"He'll be hot, he'll also be pretty pissed off I should imagine" said Jacques. "Just listen to him".

The bull could hear them talking, and he wanted to be let out of that stuffy van.

The men looked at each other; no one had any bright ideas. There was no phone number for the farm on the card, and no time of collection. It looked as if they were stuck with the bull for the time being.

The doors on the far side of the goods shed were slid shut and firmly locked in place. The few boxes of goods that were in the shed were carried to the station building where they would be safer, and then some hurdles were placed on the loading bank between the goods shed door and the door of the van in the hope that the bull would just go straight into the shed, where they had put a bucket of cold water. Carefully, using a broom to push it, Jacques began to slide open the van door. He got it half way open when pandemonium broke out; the bull charged out of the van, but instead of going into the goods shed he wanted freedom…..he could smell the sea and see the blue sky, he was off! The bull veered to the right, Henri and the guard leapt to one side and the bull careered down the slope of the loading platform with one of the hurdles around its neck. It charged along the front of the station building, and then it saw the locomotive of the goods train which had filled up with water and was now heading back slowly towards the station. The bull didn't like the locomotive; it had had enough of railways for one day. The freedom of the station approach road beckoned; the bull headed up the slope to the top of the approach road and turned left into the main street, with Jacques and the others in close….but not too close….pursuit.

It was June, it was a nice sunny day, and St Jean sur Mer was doing good business. The cafes were full, with more customers at the tables outside, and the shops were doing a good trade from locals and tourists alike. It was a prosperous scene, an orderly scene, a scene that nothing was likely to disrupt.

Then the bull got to the top of the station approach road. It had discarded the remains of the hurdle; unencumbered, it lowered its head and let out a bellow. For a moment, it was as though the world had stopped turning; there was silence…..but not for long. Someone screamed, the bull saw red curtains flapping at the open windows of a Café and he was off up the main street, scattering tables and chairs as he went. The bull didn't want any trouble, he just wanted grass beneath his feet but in the meantime he was causing chaos. One horn had picked up a rather fetching yellow & blue table cloth, on the other was a canvas bag with a teddy bear looking out of the top…truth be told, a rather concerned looking teddy bear. With the station staff flagging rather in the heat, the bull paused briefly at a grocers shop to help himself from the display for fruit and veg, then leaving a rather large deposit on the pavement in return he was off again. The main street of St Jean is quite steep, and from the top there is an excellent view across the estuary and the fields alongside it. The bull reached this point, saw the fields, let out a bellow of triumph and headed down the hill towards them. It was unfortunate that the street here is extremely narrow, and that along it in the opposite direction was coming a large cattle truck; it was the farmer coming to collect his bull from the station. The truck stopped; the farmer rubbed his eyes in disbelief, he hadn't expected his bull to be delivered straight to him. The bull couldn't get past the truck so he turned round and headed back in the direction he had just come from. The people in the main street were just recovering from the shock and congratulating themselves on having survived the experience when here it came again, looking even more wild and angry. The table cloth had gone, the teddy bear had bailed out but the canvas bag was still flapping in the slipstream as the bull charge down the middle of the street again. He didn't stop for refreshments this time, he kept on going until he came back to the station; he knew that place, he wasn't going back there again. He turned left instead.

St Jean sur Mer was in uproar; it was fortunate that no one had been hurt. Jacques and his colleagues staggered panting to the end of the main street; that bull had more stamina than they did, that was for sure. Stopping to catch their breath they could hear shouting from round the corner; when they got there the bull had finally decided to have a rest as well and was standing on the lawn of the Priest's house contentedly eating his prize roses. It was a simple matter to close the garden gate and the bull was trapped, safely enclosed until the farmer could catch up with them in his cattle truck. When he did, it was backed up to the gate and the bull was lead inside by the farmer as though it was the most placid animal in the world, and what on earth was all the fuss about?

It took a long time for the town to be restored to something resembling normality; it took a lot longer for Jacques to explain to the Gendarmes, the Mayor, the Priest and M. Artois what had happened, and how none of it was in any way his fault. By the time he got back to the station the goods train had gone, Henri and Michel had put the goods shed back as it should be, and it was time to lock up for the night. He sat down in his office for a few minutes; Mme Pinot had found seven discrepancies in his accounts that she would like to speak to him about, but somehow it didn't seem to matter. Jacques knew two things at that moment; exercise was over rated, and he needed a glass of wine. It would be purely medicinal!

Chapter 14

THE AUTORAIL EXPIRES

Jacques was becoming used to seeing the Auotrail come growling into the station on the first train of the day from Verton; at that time in the morning the holidaymakers were not up and around so there was ample room in the Autorail for the few passengers likely to need to travel. Later in the day it would be a different matter, but Jacques did worry about what would happen at the end of the holiday season when St Jean tended to hibernate through the winter months. Passengers would be a lot thinner on the ground then, and he knew in his heart of hearts that diesel railcars were the future, might indeed be the only way the railway itself might survive.

He still didn't like them, though!

On this Friday in July, almost two weeks after the visit of 'Les Anglais' had brought unheard of numbers to travel on the railway, things were back to normal. The Autorail left Verton at 09.00 and trundled into St Jean station twenty minutes later with the few people needing to do business in the town at that time on a Saturday morning. It left ten minutes later for Le Crotoy where it would stay until it formed the evening train back to Verton.

Jacques walked outside at quarter past nine to await the arrival of the train and to enjoy the breeze blowing across the estuary; St Jean harbour was looking lovely, the gulls wheeling and crying in the blue sky with only a few small white clouds scudding in the breeze. There were worse places to work than this, Jacques thought to himself, though he carefully avoided looking at the harbour office which was still covered in scaffolding after it's encounter with the two runaway vans.

He heard the sound of the Autorail's horn as it crossed the trestle bridge, and a moment later there it was running over the points and into the station, trailing the new 'remorque' trailer behind it for the boxes of shellfish. The autorail ground to a halt on the centre road and a few passengers got off, enough to keep the service viable at least. Jacques collected the tickets, and was about to walk back into the station when the driver of the Autorail called to him.

"A moment, Monsieur le Chef. I think we may have a problem".

He had opened the engine cover in the front of the vehicle, and was peering with a grim face at the diesel engine inside. As he did so there was a loud gurgling noise and a large pool of black oil appeared between the rails, seeping into the gaps between the granite setts that filled the area between the tracks to give a flat surface.

"Merde!" cried the driver, "That's all I need. Ever since they made me pull that damn trailer she's been overheating, and this has been the last straw. She's knackered!".

"But you can't leave it there!" Jacques blurted out, "How do you expect me to operate the station with one line blocked? And what about the train to Le Crotoy?".

Already people were arriving and optimistically climbing aboard the Autorail. It was no good, though, the Autorail wasn't going anywhere.

It was a sound that alerted Jacques to the solution, a sound from the engine shed; the sound of escaping steam. Louis and Maurice were in the shed preparing their loco for the morning goods train which dawdled along the line in between the passenger trains shunting at all the sidings & stations along the way. If steam was escaping from the safety valves, the loco must be ready; could she pull the Autorail?

Since the episode with the boxes of fish the Autorail had been fitted with proper couplings and a centre buffer just like the rest of the stock, so couldn't it be used just as a coach, with a steam loco pulling it? Jacques looked at the driver, the driver looked at Jacques, and as one man they took off towards the engine shed, shouting for Louis.

Louis wasn't used to his careful and leisurely preparations being interrupted but he put down his oil can and came around the front buffer beam to see what all the commotion was about. Once the situation had been explained, he said that he needed another ten minutes, the oiling round could not be rushed, but then he would be ready. The Autorail driver went back to tell the passengers what was happening, and Jacques went to telephone Verton to do the same........the departure would be delayed, but they might be able to make up some time on the way to Le Crotoy and the other trains should not be too badly affected.

Ten minutes later, a rather grimy tank engine rolled out of the shed and backed onto the front of the Autorail, after first filling its tanks to the brim at the water tower. Her sudden elevation from the local goods to a passenger train meant that there would be no time for prolonged water stops en route, and they had piled the coal bunker high with briquettes as well just in case. Louis and Maurice fully intended to enjoy their day in the limelight, and Maurice had even found time to give the loco's nameplates a polish; she was, fittingly, number two, the 'Le Crotoy'.

The driver of the Autorail put the gearbox into neutral, and settled into his seat; there was nothing more he could do other than enjoy the ride even though technically he was in charge of the train. He certainly didn't intend to get filthy on the footplate of the tank engine, not that there was really room for three there anyway. More importantly he was also the guard of the Autorail and his place was with the passengers.

Fifteen minutes later than scheduled, the loco gave a deep whistle and the makeshift train jerked into motion, very carefully and at a reduced speed as the brakes on the loco and the Autorail could not be connected so only the steam loco was able to brake the train. Off over the trestle bridge to the junction with the Verton line they chugged, there swinging south towards Rue, Quend and finally Le Crotoy where the next train would be waiting to leave. Normally during the Summer the Autorail stayed at Le Crotoy during the day, so as soon as the train was gone Jacques rang his counterpart at Le Crotoy station to tell him what to expect and to suggest that he got the local garage to send out someone who knew about diesel engines. The number two would stay for the time being in case it was needed to pull the evening train; no doubt Louis and Maurice could find something to do, paddling or building sand castles!

Now Jacques had the daily goods to think about, it had no engine but they had loaded wagons waiting to leave.............in the end he rang Verton again and they sent down the Locotracteur coupled in front of the engine on the next passenger train.

It was one advantage of diesels, Jacques had to admit, they didn't take long to get ready for use.

As far as St Jean was concerned, then, all was well, and other than spreading sand on the patch of spilled oil Jacques felt that he could relax over a cup of coffee.

The remainder of the day passed in the normal way, the only excitement being a child who had tripped over a point lever and needed patching up in the waiting room. Then late in the afternoon Jacques got a phone call from Le Crotoy; the man from the garage hadn't been able to do anything, to repair the Autorail the engine would have to be lifted out and that needed the workshops at Verton. It was returning as it had arrived, pulled ignominiously by the little steam engine. It would be running late, but it would get there in due course.

In his usual way Jacques stood outside the station building when the train was due, chatting to the few passengers waiting to return to Verton. Finally, the distant whistle could be heard as the train reached the junction, and another, closer now, as it crossed the trestle bridge.

When the strange ensemble drew into the station, a gasp arose from the waiting passengers, because during the day a transformation had taken place. With time on their hands at Le Crotoy, Loius and Maurice had not gone paddling, they had devoted themselves to cleaning and polishing their engine until it gleamed, fit at last to pull a passenger train. The red paintwork glowed in the low evening sunlight, the steel coupling and connecting rods gleamed, burnished with oil, and the brass work shone; the old engine looked a picture.

Jacques was overwhelmed, he loved the little steam loco's and to see one looking like this after all the years of minimal maintenance and little cleaning made his heart swell with pride. He wished he'd got his camera with him.

The loco uncoupled and trundled down the headshunt to run round the Autorail, and with a toot on the whistle backed along the loop past the station building. It must have been like this in the old days, thought Jacques, when all the engines looked like this.

Time was pressing, and as soon as the loco was coupled up the train was ready to leave. Jacques gave a blow on this whistle, and with Louis waving from the cab off set towards Verton.

The efforts of Louis and Maurice clearly hadn't gone unnoticed by the management, as until the Autorail was repaired the 'Le Crotoy' worked the morning and evening passenger trains as the regular engine, and she was kept immaculate while she did so. Louis and Maurice were given a small bonus in their pay packets at the end of the week in recognition of their efforts; it had been good for the railway, a lot of people had taken notice and commented favourably to the staff at Verton.

Of course, as soon as the Autorail had been repaired it was put back into use; the opportunity had been taken to replace the diesel engine with a more powerful unit that could cope with pulling the trailer, so some good came out of the incident in the end.

What really pleased Jacques, though, was the copy of 'La Vie du Rail' which a friend showed him, with a colour picture of the 'Le Crotoy' in all her glory on the front cover. Jacques immediately bought a copy and had it framed, and it has hung in a prominent position the booking office ever since.

Chapter 15

BASTILLE DAY

Bastille Day - July 14th - was approaching, and the town council of St Jean sur Mer had decided that this year a special effort must be made to make the town look attractive for the visitors. To this end, as well as the usual fireworks, procession, etc. there was to be a competition for the best decorated business in the town with a modest cash prize for the winners.

Word had come from Verton that the station was expected to take part in the competition, the railway must be seen to be playing its part in the celebrations and in boosting the image of the town. What was remarkable was that Jacques was authorised to spend a sum of money on the decorations, a small sum of money but money nevertheless. This called for serious thought; Jacques called Madame Jules into his office that afternoon as being a woman she would certainly understand these things better than he did. Jaques explained what was expected of them, and that if they won they, the staff at the station, could keep the winnings. This magnanimous gesture said a great deal of how well Verton expected them to do, but to Jacques it was as though the money was already theirs. All they had to do was decide how to decorate the station.

Madame Jules talked to her friend Madame Artur who worked in the booking office in the mornings, and they both had a chat on the telephone with the lady in the booking office at Verton station.

On the railway they had one great advantage; their many regular customers came from all walks of life, and among them were many useful contacts. Jacques began to be friendly with the passengers, most unlike him, and to be seen around the goods shed from time to time when deliveries were being made or collected. It didn't do any harm to remind people how useful the railway was to them, people who, for instance, might have a few ribbons spare or such like.

The ladies had decided that the best approach was to use flowers, planted around the station in pots & boxes; flowers in red white and blue, naturally. Flowers would last more than a few days, they wouldn't fade in the sun or blow away if the wind blew, and rain would do them good rather than damaging them. They would have some flags and ribbons too, of course, but in the main it would be done with flowers. Jacques knew better than to argue, and after all he couldn't think of anything better.

The following morning, the goods train arrived from Verton with an extra flat wagon, and on it were three old locomotive chimneys. Verton works never threw anything away; knowing this, Mme. Jules had spoken to the lady at Verton station and she had spoken to the young man in the works who rather fancied her, and here were three chimneys to use as plant pots! Jacques got the engine to put the wagon in the loading dock siding and then the two goods porters Henri and Michel to unload them from the wagon and place them wherever Mme Jules told them to when she arrived after lunch.........in the meantime, they could leave them on the barrow by the goods shed.

At half past ten a lorry arrived loaded with a dozen large earthenware pots from Quend Farm; Madame Artur told us you might like these. Some wooden window boxes followed just before lunch; truly, these women were a force to reckoned with! By three o'clock they had the window boxes in place, the three chimneys spread out along the front of the station building buried in the gravel surface to keep them upright, and the plant pots had been placed outside the station facing the road.

The plants to put in the various pots shouldn't be a problem; Madame Jules' eldest daughter Marie worked at the nursery on the Fort Mahon road, and she was going to sort out some nice specimen for them to collect in the railway lorry tomorrow morning, with some bags of peat as well. Jacques was starting to enjoy himself, especially as the ladies were doing all the work and he was getting the credit. Perhaps they should keep the flowers after Bastille Day, right through the Summer even, he pondered - why not?

The following day the plants arrived, and the ladies spent a pleasant couple of hours being creative and artistic. Mme Jules had come down to the station to help Mme Artur in the morning, while Jacques kept things ticking over inside selling the tickets, manning the telephone and making the coffee. The ladies certainly weren't going to let him anywhere near the plants! By lunch time all the pots and boxes were full to bursting, a riot of red white & blue. They had three days until the competition, by which time the flowers should have rooted well and be in full bloom. That would give them ample time to put up the finishing touches of the ribbons, flags and bunting on the walls of the station.

"One thing worries me", Mme Jules commented over a well-earned lunch in the Cafe. "How do we stop our lovely flowers being eaten by slugs?"

"Ah, that I do know!" said Jacques, "We use sea weed around the bottom of the plants. Slugs hate the salt, they won't come near. Leave it to me, that is a job I can do this afternoon".

So it was that between trains that afternoon Jacques could be seen with his trousers rolled up and his shoes & socks on the quayside, collecting seaweed from the edge of the harbour in a bucket. He was thoroughly enjoying himself; it was just like being a boy again! He spread the seaweed along the tops of the plant pots & boxes, and arranged the leaves neatly again so that it was all but invisible; a good job done. At five o'clock he and Madame Jules stood on the quayside looking at the station....they knew the competition was fierce, a lot of the businesses in the town had gone to a lot of trouble. None of them though had the space that they had here at the station, space which they had put to excellent use. Wait until tomorrow when all the other decorations were in place, they would be unbeatable!

When Jacques locked up the station later that evening, he couldn't help feeling rather pleased with himself, it had been an excellent days work. Bring on the Judges, we are ready for them.

Jacques was usually at the station by about half past eight in the morning, in good time to open up before the first train arrived from Verton. As he walked down the Rue des Moulins in the morning sunshine, he was sizing up the opposition. To be fair, a lot of the shops looked pretty impressive, they had quite inventive displays....maybe they would need to do a little more at the station after all. He pondered the possibilities as he rounded the corner into the station approach road. The flowers looked magnificent; there had been rain in the night, just the right amount, and now the drops were glistening on the leaves in the low sunlight. He unlocked the station doors, picked up the post from the mat and went into his office. Humming, he unlocked the doors to the platform and got out the cash box ready for Madame Artur who would be arriving at any time. "What an excellent morning", he thought to himself.

Jacques was jolted out of these pleasant thoughts by a scream from outside on the platform followed by the sound of running feet and the door slamming against the wall. Madame Artur flung open his office door, panting.

"The flowers! What on earth has happened to the flowers?".

"Madame, calm down, please" Jacques said, "What do you mean? The flowers look magnificent, I have just been admiring them."

"But they've gone, every last one of them! The pots and boxes are all empty, not a leaf left!" Madame Artur gasped, and dragging Jacques by the arm she pulled him out of the front of the station, the railway side. "Look!"

Jacques looked; she was right! On this side of the building, nothing remained but the bare peat. Even the seaweed had gone! What could have happened? On the road side of the station all was well, but here.......

Madame Artur went to telephone Madame Jules with the bad news while Jacques went out to deal with the approaching train. There was a lot of sympathy from the passengers when they saw what had happened, everyone gathering round to look at the empty pots, but no one had much idea of what could have happened. Then pushing through the crowd came Old Francois, the oldest fisherman in St Jean sur Mer and knowledgeable about everything to do with the river and everything that lived on or in it. The people drew to one side willingly; Old Francois carried a bit of an aroma about him. He sucked on his pipe noisily, scrubbed the stubble on his chin and then cackled loudly.

"They've gone then, 'ave they? Thought they would when I saw 'ee planting 'em".

"By how?" cried Jacques, "They were fine when we left them last night! It wasn't those young lads from the Rue St Valery was it?"

"Geese!" cried Old Francois triumphantly, "Geese! I saw 'ee, putting seaweed around 'em. As soon as you back was turned, every goose on the Authie was up here having a feast; first the seaweed, then your flowers, they had the lot. I watched 'em; took 'em half an hour, that's all. Geese! Hah!"

And with that off he walked towards his boat, still cackling.

This was a serious business; Bastille Day was tomorrow and all they had left were the earthenware pots of flowers on the road side of the station.

. Madame Jules arrived looking flustered, and when it had all been explained to her they held a council of war. The first thing they agreed was that the seaweed on balance, while well intentioned, had not been a good idea and Jaques was sent to remove it from the surviving plant pots. They would just have to take their chances with the slugs.

Second, Madame Jules got on the phone to Marie, who an hour later rang back from the Nursery to tell them to send the lorry over straight away, and that there would be no charge - this was an emergency, they must pull together! Oh, and this time sprinkle pepper over the peat in the pots, said Marie, that will keep the geese off. Madame Artur went into town to buy as much pepper as she could find.

"Take some money from the petty cash", said Jaques, "Marie is right, this is an emergency".

Finally came Jacques great idea; when he shared it with the two ladies they were, he was amazed to find, full of enthusiasm, in fact so much so that they told him to get on the phone to Verton straight away, waste no time! So that is what he did.

By early afternoon they had replaced all the plants and the station was looking colourful again; the station building was draped with bunting and flags, the work of Henri & Michel, and everything that could be swept and tidied had been. Woe betide the passenger that dropped a cigarette end on the floor today! A message had come from the Judges of the competition that they would be visiting the station at around 2pm tomorrow afternoon after doing the bulk of the town in the morning and then, of course, taking lunch.

"Good", said Jacques, "They should be feeling a bit more mellow after lunch! We will still have to get busy in the morning, though, if we are going to be ready on time".

At eight thirty on the morning of the 14th all three of them were at the station to open up an make sure all was in order. Thankfully, the flowers that had been planted yesterday were all in place and looking wonderful so that was once concern less, they could concentrate on the Piece de Resistance!

They went outside at eight thirty to await the arrival of the first train of the day from Verton, which in the Tourist season was still steam hauled. Today though, it had not one but two locomotives at the front and the leading one was the 'Authie', old Number One, sparkling in the sunshine as though it was brand new; someone at Verton had done them proud! Louis and Maurice were grinning at them from the footplate; they had stayed with friends in Verton last night to make sure that they would be in charge of the spare loco which would otherwise have stayed in the shed at St Jean. It was uncoupled from the train and backed onto the loading dock shed siding where it wouldn't interfere with the normal working of the station. Jacques gathered the conspirators together and explained exactly what he wanted them to do.

The morning passed quickly; there was the everyday work to be done, of course, but Jacques again looked after the station while the ladies, helped by Louis and Maurice worked their magic on the little locomotive. Just before lunch time, it was backed as far into the locomotive shed as possible and the doors were closed, leaving the engine in light steam until it was needed. None of them dared go for lunch in case the judges were early; after twelve there were no more trains for a couple of hours, so they pottered around the station tidying things that had already been tidied and generally feeling nervous. The tension rose as two o'clock approached; the train from Le Crotoy arrived in the normal way and left again at twenty past and still no sign of the judges.

"At this rate they'll be in no fit state to judge anything" Jacques commented, and at that moment a small procession of smartly dressed town dignitaries came round the corner from the Rue des Moulins and towards the station, all of them carrying a clip board. They greeted Jacques warmly and told him just to ignore them to carry on the normal business of the station as though they were not there. As if such a thing was possible!

Louis and Maurice were quickly sent back to the loco shed while the judges were still outside, and Madame Artur who was by now off duty stood half way between the station and the shed where Louis had a good view of her. The judges pottered about looking at the road side of the station, then came in for a look in the waiting room before walking out again into the sunlight on the platform side. The flowers were almost incandescent in the strong summer sunshine, the flags flapped in the breeze coming off the estuary and the bunting rustled. It looked lovely, but it was not enough, it did not yet have that certain something that made it stand out from the rest of the town,

Time to play the trump card!

Jacques signalled to Madame Artur, Madame Artur signalled to Louis, and there was a shriek of a locomotive whistle from inside the engine shed. The entrance to the shed filled with steam so that nothing could be seen, and then slowly, majestically through the cloud there came a vision..........the little locomotive, gleaming in the sunshine and carrying three French Tricolours on the buffer beam, bunting along the side tanks, bunting around the cab and twisted around the handrails, flowers along the tank tops and cascading from the cab roof. Whistling furiously, the loco trundled into the station and stopped on the quayside right opposite the judges, who were standing spellbound in front of the booking hall door. With a final triumphant toot on the whistle Louis and Maurice climbed down from the footplate, each with a flower in their cap and a button hole on their overalls.

Not a word was spoken for a good thirty seconds. Jacques himself was beyond speech; he had tears in his eyes. Then one of the Judges spoke; "Formidable, Monsieur. Formidable!

I congratulate you! Don't move it, I am going home to get my camera!"

The train from Verton pulled into the station, and soon a crowd of people were clustered around the 'Authie'. What's more, Monsieur Artois himself had come over on the train to see how they had done and he came across to shake Jacques hand. The local newspaper had sent their photographer down and Louis and Maurice were acting like two film stars, hanging off the footplate with big silly grins on their faces.

"Excellent, Jacques, excellent, "M. Artois was saying, "Wonderful publicity for the railway, just what we need. I am delighted, and what's more it hasn't cost much; what could be better?".

The rest of the day passed in a blur; at six o'clock it was announced at the gathering in the town square that the winner of the Decorated Business prize was St Jean station. Jacques collected the prize envelope from Monsieur the Mayor, and the evening was spent by himself, Louis, Maurice, Henri, Michel and of course Madames Artur and Jules putting the prize money to good use in the Cafe Pierre.............well, they began in the Cafe Pierre! That evening there were fireworks, there was dancing, and the whole of St Jean came to life celebrating until the early hours of the morning.

The following day was quieter - Jaques was certainly a great deal quieter than usual - as the locomotive was stripped if its finery and returned to Verton at the front of the morning goods train after being serviced by Louis and Maurice. The bunting and the flags came down, but the flowers were to stay, M. Artois had been most impressed with that idea and was going to suggest that the other stations on the railway did the same.

What made it all perfect was the phone call from M. Artois that afternoon. He had been talking to the Mayor.

"t's about the 'Authie', Jacques" Said M. Artois, "I sent her up yesterday but she's not really capable of any hard work anymore. She is the engine that pulled the first train on the railway in 1898, I can't bring myself to have her scrapped."

"Sentiment - from M.Artois?" thought Jacques, "He must be mellowing in his old age!"

"I have been talking to the Mayor of St Jean. The Mayor is going to have a piece of ground prepared in the station approach, and a length of track will be laid. We are presenting the 'Authie' to the town of St Jean sur Mer, Jacques, as a reminder of the important part our railway has played in the development of the town. We will have the engine fully restored here in the works, then we will make arrangements for bringing her over to you. The mayor has promised a proper ceremony, and I want you to do the unveiling Jacques".

With that, M. Artois rang off. Jacques replaced the receiver in its cradle and sat at his desk for a long time without moving.............and this time it wasn't just due to his hangover.

Chapter 16

THE 'AUTHIE' RESTORED

On Bastille Day 1998, the Reseau de Cote de Picardie celebrated it's centenary with the first steaming of the restored No 1 'Authie', which had been removed from the plinth where it had been standing since 1958, taken into the workshops at Verton and made as good as new.

It was the highlight of the steam festival weekend that had brought thousands of visitors to St Jean and which would become a bi-annual event, boosting the economy of the town and the status of the preservation society that had taken over the CdP system in in 1972 when the last freight trains had been withdrawn. The ensuing years hadn't been easy but now the railway was a major tourist attraction which was recognised by the Picardie department with funding and support.

The Mayoress of St Jean sur Mer, Marianne Dupont, who had been Marianne Charles back in 1958, broke a bottle of Champagne over the front buffer of the little Corpet Louvet to christen it and the celebrations began...never had the little town entertained so many people. The people who kept the railway going through the difficult times when there was no money to spare may have gone but their spirit lived on in the enthusiastic volunteers who manned the same station now.

No 1 gave a toot on the whistle and pulled out of St Jean sur Mer station with the first train of the day to Verton—celebrations were all very well but there was still a timetable to be kept to.

GLOSSARY

CORPET LOUVET   A maker of locomotives widely used on French narrow gauge railways.

AUTORAIL   A diesel or petrol powered railcar.

LOCOTRACTEUR   A small diesel locomotive, often built on the chassis of a withdrawn steam engine.

FOURGON   A guards van used on passenger trains which also carried luggage and small goods.

CHEF DE GARE   Station master

REMORQUE   A small trailer puller by an Autorail.

S.N.C.F.   The French national railway system, created in 1938.

The photographs in this book have been used to illustrate the story, but are not intended to be an accurate representation of the scene...they were taken by the author on the Baie de Somme and the Vivarais railways.

You might enjoy these other books by Peter Smith:

THE ANNECY TO THONES TRAMWAY

THE THIZY TRAMWAY

MAYENNE NARROW GAUGE

NARROW GAUGE IN THE DROME & VAUCLUSE

THE CHEMINS DE FER DE LA MANCHE

NARROW GAUGE ON THE COTE DU NORD

NARROW GAUGE RAILWAYS OF FINISTERE

THE RAILWAYS OF CHARLEVILLE MEZIERES AND THE FRENCH ARDENNES

THE SARTHE TRAMWAYS

FRENCH MINOR RAILWAYS VOLS 1, 2 AND 3.

NARROW GAUGE ON THE ILE DE RE.

THE RAILWAYS OF HAUTE SAVOIE

Printed in Great Britain
by Amazon